Cupcake

Mia's
Boiling Point

Coco Simon

First published in Great Britain in 2013 by
Simon and Schuster UK Ltd
A CBS COMPANY

Originally published in the USA in 2012 by Simon Spotlight,
an imprint of Simon & Schuster Children's Division, New York.

Copyright © 2012 by Simon and Schuster, Inc.
Text by Tracey West.
Design by Laura Roode.

Simon & Schuster UK Ltd
1st Floor,
222 Gray's Inn Road,
London
WC1X 8HB

Simon & Schuster Australia, Sydney
Simon & Schuster India, New Delhi

This book is a work of fiction. Names, characters, places and incidents
are either the product of the author's imagination or are used fictitiously.
Any resemblance to actual people living or dead,
events or locales is entirely coincidental.

A CIP catalogue record for this book is available from the British Library.

PB ISBN 978-1-47111-634-6
eBook ISBN 978-1-47111-635-3

1 3 5 7 9 10 8 6 4 2

Printed and bound in Great Britain by CPI Group (UK) Ltd, Croydon, CR0 4YY

www.simonandschuster.co.uk
www.simonandschuster.com.au

CHAPTER 1

A Middle School Miracle?

Oh my gosh, it's a cupcake plunger!" my friend Katie squealed.

I don't think I've ever seen Katie so excited. We were in a shop called Baker's Hollow. They sell baking supplies, and inside are all these fake trees with built-in shelves and the supplies are displayed on them.

Katie and I were at the cupcake tree, which has pretty, fake pink cupcakes "growing" in its fake branches. The shelves are filled with cupcake baking pans, cupcake decorations, and tons of different kinds of cupcake liners.

Katie was holding up a metal tube with a purple top on it. She pulled on the top, and it moved up and down, like a plunger.

"This is so cool!" she cried. "You stick this in the top of the cupcake and plunge down halfway, and a perfect little tube of cake comes out. Then you fill the hole with stuff and then put the cake back on top and frost it. Just imagine what you could put in here! Whipped cream! Pudding!"

She turned to me, and her brown eyes were shining with excitement. "You could even do ice cream! Can you imagine biting into a cupcake and there's ice cream inside? How awesome would that be?"

"Totally awesome," I agreed. "Plus, it's purple. Your favourite colour."

Katie dug into her pocket, took out some crumpled notes, and started to count.

"It's only six pounds. I could get it and still have enough left over for a smoothie," she said, and then she sighed. "I am so glad they opened this store, but I am going to go broke spending all my money on cupcake supplies. I'm obsessed!"

"I know how you feel," I said. "I am totally obsessed with shoes lately. I'm trying to find the perfect pair of neutral heels. I want them dressy, but not too dressy – maybe a shiny patent leather, with a high heel. But not too high. I don't want to fall flat on my face! I can picture them in my mind, but I haven't seen them anywhere for real yet."

Katie looked down at her trainers, which were decorated with rainbows drawn on with pen. "I don't think I'll ever wear heels. They're too uncomfortable."

That's the difference between Katie and me – she doesn't care about fashion at all, and I pretty much live for it. Today, for instance, Katie was wearing a purple hoodie, jeans and trainers. Which is perfectly adorable on her, but not dressed up enough for me. You never know who you could run into at the shops! So I had on skinny black jeans, my furry black boots, a white lace cami and a sky-blue cardigan on top. The beads in my hoop earrings matched my cardigan, and the boho style of the earrings worked perfectly with my boots.

But even though Katie doesn't care much about fashion, she's my best friend here in Maple Grove. I moved here a year ago after my parents got divorced. Katie was the first friend I met.

"Okay, I'd better get on line before I buy something else," she told me.

A few minutes later we left the shop, and Katie was happily holding an adorable little paper shopping bag with a picture of a cupcake tree on it.

"That's such a great logo," I said. "I wish I had thought of that for the Cupcake Club."

"I bet you could think of an even better logo if you wanted to," Katie said.

That made me feel pretty good. I love to draw and would love to be a fashion designer or maybe a graphic designer one day. Or maybe one of those designers who does displays in store windows in Manhattan. How cool would that be?

As we walked towards the smoothie shop, the smell of chocolate distracted us. Katie and I didn't even need to discuss it. We walked right into Adele's Chocolates and headed for the counter.

This is a "must-go-to" shop. Adele makes all the chocolates herself, and the flavours are amazing.

"Mmm, look," I said, pointing to a glistening morsel of chocolate in a gold paper cup. "Salted caramel. That sounds so good."

Katie pointed to a piece of dark chocolate sitting in a pale purple cup. "Dark chocolate infused with lavender. I wonder what that tastes like?"

"That would make a good cupcake," I said, and Katie nodded. We talk about cupcakes a lot because we're in the Cupcake Club with our friends Alexis and Emma. It's a real business. People hire us to bake for their parties and other events.

Katie had a pained look on her face. "Soooo tempting. But I think I really need some smoothie energy right about now. Mum says chocolate makes me loopy."

I grabbed Katie's arm and pretended to drag her out of the store. "Resist! Resist!" I said, and we both started laughing like crazy.

"We should go right to the smoothie place," I said when we calmed down. "No more distractions."

"Right," Katie said. She stood up straight, like a soldier, and saluted. "To the smoothie place!"

It was Saturday, so the shops were pretty crowded as we made our way to Smoothie Paradise. I used to hate the shops when I first moved here, because I was so used to shopping in New York City. But now I like it. It's never too hot or too cold, and when I'm done shopping I just have to carry the bags outside to Mum's car. It's definitely a lot easier than toting things home on the train.

Even though the shops were full of people, the line at Smoothie Paradise was pretty short. Katie and I each ordered the same thing — a smoothie with mango and passion fruit — and then sat down at a small round table in the corner.

"This is my favourite kind of day," Katie said

after taking a long slurp from her straw. "I got all my homework done last night, so I don't have anything to worry about."

I nodded. "Me too."

Katie sat back in her chair. "You know, middle school isn't so bad so far. I mean, it's not perfect, but I think it's easier this year."

"Definitely," I agreed. "It's, like, we know our way around. And besides school, other things are easier too. Like living with Eddie and Dan. That's not so weird anymore."

Eddie is my stepdad, and Dan is my stepbrother. They're both pretty nice.

"Is it getting any easier living in two different apartments?" Katie asked.

I thought about it for a minute. "Yeah, kind of," I admitted. "But mostly when I go to my dad's, I feel like I'm visiting." I basically go out to New York to see my dad every other weekend.

"You must miss him," Katie said.

I wasn't sure how to answer that. Katie's parents are divorced too, and she never sees her dad. He remarried, and I think he even has a whole new family. So as tough as my situation is, I think Katie's is even tougher.

I decided to be honest. "Sometimes I miss him,"

I said. "But he texts me and Skypes me and stuff during the week. So he's there if I need him."

Katie got a little quiet after I said that, so I changed the subject.

"We should go to Icon after this," I said. Katie knows that's my favourite clothing store. "They sell shoes there, too. Maybe they have my perfect heels."

We left the shop and headed for Icon. It's easy to find because you can hear techno music blasting from it even when the mall is noisy. The decor is really sleek and clean, with white walls and gleaming silver racks. I like it that way because the clothes are really highlighted.

That day I walked right past the clothes and headed straight for the shoes, which were displayed on white blocks sticking out of the back wall. They had chunky heels, wedge heels and spike heels, but the perfect shoe, the one I could picture in my head, wasn't there.

While I was looking at all the shoes, Katie was giggling and wobbling in a pair of superhigh silver heels. I suddenly heard a familiar voice behind us.

"Hi, Mia. Hi, Katie."

It was Callie Wilson, Katie's former best friend and the leader of the Best Friends Club, which used to be the Popular Girls Club. Things have always been pretty tense between the Cupcake Club and the BFC. A lot of it had to do with Katie and Callie's broken friendship. But recently, they kind of patched things up, and so today Callie was smiling and friendly.

Katie, on the other hand, looked a little startled. She quickly slipped out of the silver heels, embarrassed.

"Oh, hey, Callie," Katie said.

"Hi," I added.

Maggie and Bella, the other two girls in the BFC, walked up behind Callie. Maggie has wild hair and can be pretty funny when she wants to be – and pretty mean, too. Bella is the quietest of the three. She's super into those vampire movies – like, so into them that she changed her name from Brenda to Bella, and she straightens her auburn hair to look just like the girl who loves the vampire.

"Shopping for shoes?" Callie asked, even though it was pretty obvious. I guess she was trying to make conversation.

"I'm trying to find the perfect pair of heels," I said. "But I think they only exist in my head."

"Ooh, I saw this adorable pair online," Maggie said. She whipped out her smartphone and started typing on the keyboard. Then she shoved the screen in front of my face. "See?"

"Those are totally cute, but the ones I'm dreaming of have a pointier toe," I told her. "But thanks!"

"Did you guys see those new wrap dresses they got in?" Callie asked. "Katie, there's a purple one that would look so cute on you."

"We'll definitely check them out," I replied.

"Yeah," Katie added.

Callie gave a little wave and then flipped her long, blonde hair over her shoulder. "Okay, we've got to go. Later."

She walked away, and Bella and Maggie followed her. Katie and I stared at each other in shock.

"Did that just actually happen?" Katie asked.

"You mean, did we actually just have a normal conversation with the BFC, with no name-calling or teasing? Yes!" I replied.

Katie grinned. "It's a middle school miracle!"

CHAPTER 2

The Shoes of My Dreams

On Sunday morning when I woke up, the house smelled like bacon. As far as I'm concerned, that is the absolute best way to wake up.

I got dressed and went downstairs to find Mum and Eddie in the kitchen. There was a big plate of bacon on the table, and Eddie was flipping pancakes at the stove.

"She's alive!" Eddie said, teasing me. I looked at the clock, and it was ten thirty.

"Hey, it's still morning," I said. "Besides, I don't see Dan."

Dan is in high school, and he sleeps way more than I do. I was pretty sure Dan must still be asleep.

I was right. "He's still sleeping," Mum said. She had her long, black hair pulled back with a big barrette. People say I look like my mum, but it's mostly my hair; I definitely have my dad's nose, and our faces are both oval. Mum's is more heart shaped.

"Too bad! That means more bacon for us," Eddie said cheerfully.

"Ed, that's not nice. We should save him some," Mum scolded.

Eddie put a platter of pancakes on the table and gave my mum a kiss. (Gross.) "Of course I will, *mi amore*. You know I have a soft heart."

"That's why I married you," Mum said, and I made a loud coughing noise.

"Excuse me! Child present!" I reminded them.

Eddie hugged my mum. "You'll understand one day, Mia, when you're in love."

"Okay, now I am seriously losing my appetite," I said. I like Eddie and everything, but deep down I still wish my mum and dad were together. So I don't need to see Mum and Eddie all lovey-dovey.

Mum gave Eddie a look, and he stopped hugging her and sat down at the table. "Pancakes, anyone?"

"Me, please," I said. "And bacon."

While Eddie piled the food onto my plate, Mum said, "Mia, I know I've been working a lot lately, so I was thinking maybe we could have a girls' day

11

out today. Unless you have other plans with your friends."

I put down my fork. "Can we go to the city? Hang out in SoHo? And get Thai food? And go window shopping? When can we leave?"

Even though I stay with my dad in Manhattan every other weekend, I hardly ever get to go with my mum. I miss the things we used to do there together.

Mum smiled. "I don't see why not. We should leave after breakfast. We can take the ferry."

So less than two hours later we were standing on the top deck of a ferry crossing the Hudson River. It was a pretty chilly out, but I didn't mind because I got to wear a new fall jacket that one of my mum's designer friends had given her. It's cobalt blue, and it has a vintage-style collar that looks like two petals, and three big buttons in the front, and it's fitted around the waist, with a belt and a big buckle.

I wore it with black knit tights and this navy shirtdress I have, which was from another one of my mum's friends. Mum's a fashion stylist, so I am superlucky and can get great clothes for free.

Mum was going for the all-black look, which she does a lot. Black jumper, black knee-length skirt, black tights, black boots, black trench coat. I call it her spy outfit.

"Yes, but I can always accessorise," Mum loves to say, and she can make it look different every time with a bright red scarf or a big silver necklace or a belt or something. She's good at that.

When the ferry docked we took a cab to SoHo, a neighbourhood in Manhattan that stands for "south of Houston," which is Houston Street (only people pronounce it "*how*-ston" instead of "*hyoo*-ston," like the city in Texas). There are other places to shop in New York City, like great department stores, but I think SoHo is fun because the streets are narrow and lots of designers have little shops there. New stores are always springing up, so you never know what you'll see.

We were extremely full from the pancakes and bacon, so we went window shopping first. A lot of the clothing boutiques had winter coats on display already. We admired a shop with some pretty cool faux-fur jackets and then moved on to the next store.

I froze. The window was filled with the most amazing shoes I had ever seen. The sign above the door read KARA KAREN.

"She must have just opened up the boutique,"

Mum said. "Everyone's saying great things about her."

I grabbed Mum by the arm. "We are going inside!" I informed her.

Mum didn't argue. A bell jingled as we walked inside the shop, a clean, well-lit space with polished wood floors. The shoes were displayed on a round table in the centre of the shop with different tiers, like a layer cake. My eyes scanned the display from the bottom, to the middle, to the very top layer, and that's when I saw them – my dream shoes.

The heel was high, but not too high. And it wasn't chunky, but not too spiky, either. The toe was nice and pointy, just like I wanted. The shoe itself was black, but kind of sparkly. Delicate straps crisscrossed the top of the shoe.

Mum must have noticed my wide-eyed look. Or maybe I was drooling.

"Those are great shoes," she said. "Impractical, but gorgeous."

I immediately started to appeal to Mum's fashion sense. "Mum, you know I need heels for special occasions. This is the perfect pair! They'll go with just about anything. And the heel's not too high."

Mum reached up and took the sample shoe off the stand. Then she looked at the price tag.

"How much?" I asked nervously.

"Too much," Mum said. The tag said: £212.

I was so disappointed! "I knew they were too good to be true," I said with a sigh. "I guess when I imagined my dream shoes, I should have imagined a cheaper price."

Mum was turning the shoe over in her hand, examining it with a thoughtful look on her face.

"I'll tell you what, Mia," she said. "If you can raise money for your half of the shoes, I'll pay for the other half." She laughed. "You buy one shoe and I'll buy the other!"

I immediately felt much better. "You mean we can get them now and I'll owe you?"

Mum shook her head. "No, you have to earn the money first. Then you'll appreciate them more."

I did some quick calculations in my head. I had some money saved from the Cupcake business, and I get allowance for helping around the house. I could see if maybe I could do some extra chores, and I knew the Cupcake Club had a big job coming up. It wouldn't take long . . . but just thinking about the wait was unbearable!

I took the shoe from my mum and hugged it dramatically. "I'll miss you! But I will come back for you, I promise!"

Mum laughed again. "Well, before you get carried away, we should at least try them on."

The saleswoman in the shop got the shoes in my size, and I put them on. They looked fabulous! I was a little wobbly when I walked in them, but I got the hang of it pretty quickly.

"It's that extra-pointy toe," Mum said. "But I have to admit, you're pretty good in them."

"It's in my genes," I said. When Mum walks in high heels, she's as graceful as a ballet dancer.

"We should get lunch soon," Mum said.

I looked at myself in the mirror one last time. Then I took off the shoes. I took a gazillion pictures of them with my phone camera. Then I sadly gave them back to the saleswoman.

"Good-bye," I whispered, gazing longingly at the shoes as we left the shop.

Yes, I was definitely in the middle of a shoe obsession!

CHAPTER 3

The New Girl

I couldn't stop thinking about shoes. The next morning I showed Katie my phone's pictures on the bus.

"They're nice," she said. "But they look hard to walk in."

She quickly got bored with my shoe talk, so I spent the rest of the ride trying to calculate how long it would take me to earn my half of the shoes. I was pretty fixated on this until I got to homeroom, when something happened to distract me.

A girl I had never seen before was standing inside the room by the front door. Her nervous expression was the first thing I noticed about her. The second thing I noticed, of course, was her outfit.

She was about as tall as me, with green eyes and thick brown hair that touched her shoulders and a chunky fringe across her forehead. She was wearing skinny jeans, short black boots with heels, a grey ruffled top and this cute, short, long-sleeve blue jacket. Hanging from her neck was a brass necklace with a key dangling from the end.

I walked up to her. "I like your outfit," I said, and she smiled.

"Oh, thanks!"

I would have said more, but the bell rang and our form teacher, Ms Chandar, entered. She's the science teacher, and she's always dressed very neatly, in a pressed button-down shirt, simple A-line skirt and sensible shoes. She looks like the kind of person whose house doesn't have a speck of dust in it.

"You must be Olivia," Ms Chandar said, approaching the new girl. "Please find a seat."

"There's an empty one next to me," I told Olivia, and she smiled gratefully and followed me to the back of the room.

After we said the Pledge of Allegiance and listened to the day's announcements by Principal LaCosta, Ms Chandar explained that the new girl was Olivia Allen, and she had just moved to Maple

Grove. Right away I felt totally protective of her, because I know how weird it feels to be the new girl. I got lucky, because I met Katie, Emma and Alexis on my first day of school.

So when the registration bell rang, I turned to Olivia.

"I'm Mia," I said. "If you want, you can sit with me and my friends at lunch. I'll wait for you by the cafeteria door."

Olivia smiled. "Thanks, that would be cool."

I didn't think that Katie, Emma or Alexis would mind one bit. After all, we weren't some exclusive club like the Best Friends Club used to be when Sydney Whitman was the leader and it was called the Popular Girls Club. Anyway, I had a chance to tell them during third period, because it turned out Olivia was in P. E. with us. Because she was new, Olivia didn't have any P. E. clothes with her, so she was sitting on the benches.

"Who's the new girl?" Alexis asked, nodding towards her as we came out of the changing room.

"She's in my form. Her name's Olivia. I invited her to sit with us at lunch," I said.

"That's cool," Katie said.

"Is she nice?" Emma asked.

I shrugged. "I guess. She just looked kind of sad,

and I remember what it feels like to be new, you know?"

Then Ms Chen, our P. E. teacher, blew her whistle and made us do a bunch of jumping jacks and sit-ups. Then she kept us busy playing flag football, so we didn't have much of a chance to talk again until lunch.

Olivia was already waiting by the cafeteria door when I got there. She looked pretty relieved to see me.

"Come on, I'll introduce you to my friends," I said.

"Are those the girls you were hanging out with in P. E.?" Olivia asked.

"Yes," I replied. "They're totally nice. I guarantee that you will love them."

I led her to our table in the back of the lunchroom, where Katie was unpacking her lunch bag. Emma and Alexis were waiting on the hot-lunch line, like they always do.

"Olivia, this is Katie," I said.

Katie smiled. "Hey. So where are you from?"

Olivia sat down between me and Katie. "Jersey City, right across from Manhattan," she said, sighing. "I used to be able to take a train there whenever I wanted. But now we're, like, in the middle of nowhere. There's nothing to do out here."

"I used to live in Manhattan," I told her. "And I used to feel that way too. But Maple Grove is really nice. And it's not that far from the city. I go there all the time."

Olivia's eyes got wide. "You're from Manhattan? That's totally amazing."

That's when Alexis and Emma walked up, and I introduced them both.

"Hey, so Olivia used to live right by the city," I said.

"I always thought it would be exciting to live in Manhattan," Emma said. "But then I think I'd miss the trees and parks."

"Central Park is eight hundred and forty three acres," Alexis informed her. (She loves facts and figures.) "That's a lot of trees."

"But they're all in one place," Katie pointed out. "In Maple Grove, they're all over."

I noticed that while my friends were talking, Olivia wasn't really listening. She was scanning the cafeteria, checking out everyone at the tables. I didn't really think that was rude or anything. She was probably just taking everything in.

Then we started talking Cupcake business.

"So, Katie, are we meeting at your house on

Wednesday?" Alexis asked and took out her laptop to start checking things off. She's superorganised.

Katie nodded. "Mum says it's okay."

I turned to Olivia. "We formed a Cupcake Club. It's a real business now. We make cupcakes and sell them."

Olivia didn't seem to be interested.

"Every Friday, one of us brings in cupcakes for all of us," I explained. I looked at Alexis. "I'll do the cupcakes this Friday. I'll bring in an extra for Olivia."

Alexis raised an eyebrow like she was surprised I said that, which I thought was a little weird, but then she nodded. "Okay. The four of us can talk more at our meeting on Wednesday."

I didn't see Olivia until seventh period, when we had chorus together. She sat next to me again. When school ended we figured out that she took a different bus than Katie and me.

She took out her phone. "Tell me your number, and I'll text you mine."

We quickly exchanged numbers, and then I ran to catch the bus with Katie.

"So Olivia seems pretty nice," I said as we took our seats.

"Sure," Katie said. "Only, Alexis was talking to

me at the end of lunch when you and Olivia went to the toilet. She was saying, you know, how the Cupcake Club is a business and everything and how we can't invite anyone to join the business without voting on it or whatever."

I rolled my eyes. "Alexis is such a worrier. I just asked Olivia to sit with us at lunch, that's all. I hope you guys don't have a problem with that."

"Of course not," Katie said. "We're not the PGC or the BFC or whatever. I guess Alexis just wants to keep Olivia separate from the whole Cupcake thing, you know, until we know her."

I suddenly felt suspicious. "Did Alexis ask you to talk to me about it?"

Katie absently twirled a strand of her wavy brown hair around her finger. "Yeah, well, I guess she thought you'd take it better from me."

I shook my head. "She's making a big deal out of nothing. Alexis and Emma made new friends at camp, and it was no big deal, right? We're always going to meet new people. But we're the four Musketeers. Nothing will ever break that up."

Katie grinned. "You mean, *Cupcake*teers. And, anyway, weren't there only three Musketeers?"

"Maybe, but we're Cupcaketeers, and you definitely need four of those," I said.

Katie put her hand over her heart and started to recite dramatically, "Loyal and true, through thick icing and thin icing, through runny cake mix and burned cupcake bottoms! We will stick together!" And then we laughed, like we always do.

CHAPTER 4

My New "Roommate"

I have to admit that I was curious to see what Olivia would wear on Tuesday, and I made extra-sure that I wore a cool outfit too. I went with a cute floral-print dress in dark reds and purples, which are perfect for autumn. The dress has short sleeves and, like, a puffy skirt. I wore a short black cardigan over it, unbuttoned; my black tights and my go-to black ankle boots. I checked out my reflection in the mirror. Adorable!

When I spotted Olivia that morning, her outfit didn't disappoint. She went with skinny jeans again, this time in black, and she had a blue cable-knit jumper underneath an unbuttoned short denim jacket. (She seems to like to layer her outfits, which I think always looks stylish.) What I liked best was her red flats with small black bows, because the unexpected colour contrast was fun. She also had a red headband in her glossy hair.

"Hey," I said as I slid into my seat. "Love the red shoes and headband."

"Thanks," she said, but she didn't sound happy. In fact, she looked pretty sad again. She made a big sigh, and I could sort of tell that she wanted me to ask what was wrong. So I did.

"Is everything okay?" I asked.

"It's awful!" she replied. "Principal LaCosta says there aren't any open lockers. I'm going to have to carry all my books everywhere! My arms are going to fall off!"

"Why don't you share mine?" I suggested. I definitely felt sorry for her. I couldn't imagine carrying around six classes' worth of books everywhere.

Olivia immediately perked up. "Really?"

I nodded. "Sure."

The bell hadn't rung yet, so I walked up to Ms Chandar's desk. "Olivia doesn't have a locker, so I'm going to let her share mine," I said. "Would it be okay if we put her stuff in now?"

Ms Chandar looked up from her planner. "That's very nice of you, Mia. Of course!"

I motioned to Olivia, who quickly got up. She

26

grabbed her black-and-white leopard print backpack, which looked totally stuffed, and lugged it out of the room.

My locker was just down the hallway.

"Get out your phone, and I'll give you the combination," I told her. When she was ready, I said the numbers out loud as I opened the lock. "Thirteen, twenty-six, nine."

"Got it!" Olivia said, and then her eyes got wide when I opened the door.

"Oh my gosh, Mia, this is the coolest locker ever!" she cried.

I guess I forgot to mention that as soon as school began I started designing my locker for fun. Over the summer, I sketched out the design I wanted and then shopped for the perfect materials. On the inside of the front door, I put this stick-on wallpaper with a groovy sixties design in purple, orange and green. Then I went to a carpet store, and they gave me these free carpet scraps — purple shag — that were just perfect. I put the carpet on the floor of the locker and on top of the shelf. Dangling from the shelf is this superadorable mini-chandelier that sparkles when I turn on the little battery-operated light that I stuck under the shelf.

"Thanks," I told Olivia. "Just because it's a school

27

locker doesn't mean it can't be fabulous, right?"

"It's so nice, I'm afraid to put anything in here," Olivia said.

"Well, I can fit all my books on the top shelf," I said. "I hardly put anything on the bottom anyway. So you can fit all your books there."

Olivia opened up her backpack and gave one of those big sighs I was starting to get used to. "I don't even know where to start!"

"Here, it's easy," I said. I started taking books out of her backpack and piling them in. "Just make sure you have what you need for your next class."

After the books were stacked, Olivia opened up the front pocket of her backpack. "In my old locker I could always have a mirror, so I could check my hair and stuff," she said, pulling out a round mirror. "There are stickers on the back. We could just stick it to the door."

All I could think of was my gorgeous wallpaper being ruined. "Hey, why don't we get one of those hooks that you can put on a wall and it doesn't ruin it," I suggested. "I can bring one in tomorrow."

Olivia shrugged. "Sure, I guess."

Then she pulled out this pink plastic makeup box and stuck it on top of her book pile. The pink didn't exactly go with my design, but I wanted to be nice. So I didn't say anything.

Olivia opened the box, and I saw that it was filled with different shades of lip gloss.

"Hey, is that ETX lip gloss?" I asked. "They have such cool colours."

"I got a whole set for my birthday," she said. "I'll bring you one tomorrow."

"Thanks!" I replied.

Then the homeroom bell rang, so we closed the locker.

"Yay! This is fun. It's like having a roommate," I said.

Olivia gave me a hug. "Thanks, Mia!" she said. "I honestly don't know what I would do without you."

I was feeling pretty good as I headed to my next class, and it wasn't just because I had helped out Olivia. I was sure I had made a new friend.

CHAPTER 5

Sporty but Suave?

The next morning I went to my locker before registration, and I found Olivia putting on lip gloss while looking in her mirror, which was hung on the inside door of my locker.

"Oh cool, I guess you found the special hook," I said. "I brought one too."

Olivia kept her eyes on the mirror. "Oh, I just stuck it on with the sticky pads on the back. It's just easier that way, right?"

For a second my heart sank as I imagined the holes left in my wallpaper once Olivia got her own locker. I figured she didn't understand what I had meant about the special hook that doesn't damage walls. So I didn't say anything.

"Nice colour," I complimented her. The lip gloss

she was applying was a shimmery pinkish-tan colour. I could tell she was going for a kind of neutral look today, with a tan boyfriend jacket and a white blouse underneath.

"Thanks," she said, smacking her lips one last time. Then she turned to me and smiled. "Come on, let's get to homeroom."

She put the lip gloss back in the plastic box, and for a second I remembered her promise – that she would bring me an ETX lip gloss today. But Olivia didn't mention it as we closed and locked the locker. I didn't think this was a really big deal either. She had probably just forgotten about it.

Then after second period I went to my locker before P. E. and I noticed that Olivia had stuffed some of her books on my shelf. I had to put them back down on the bottom so I could fit my stuff.

She's probably just getting used to everything, I thought.

And right now most people would probably be thinking, *Wow, Mia's making a lot of excuses for Olivia.* Which I was. But she was new, and well, none of it seemed like a big deal.

That night, we had a Cupcake Club meeting at Katie's house. Katie doesn't have any brothers or sisters, and she lives with just her mum, who's a dentist. Like Katie, Mrs Brown also loves to cook and bake things, which seems kind of weird for a dentist to like to do, but once you meet her, it's totally not weird at all. It's just who she is.

At six o'clock, Katie, Alexis, Emma and I were all sitting around Katie's kitchen table. When we meet together on a school night, we sometimes have dinner, so it doesn't interfere with homework.

Mrs Brown came to the table carrying a steaming pot of soup. She was wearing a red checkered apron that read #1 CHEF on the front.

"Black bean soup," she said, putting the pot on the table. "And Katie made some quesadillas for us."

"Katie, you are going to turn into a taco if you keep eating all this Mexican food," I teased her. She went to cooking camp over the summer, and she's been on a Mexican food kick ever since.

"Could I turn into a burrito instead?" she asked. "'Cause I like those better."

Katie's mum ladled some soup into our bowls, and we dug in, blowing on the soup to cool it off. I put some sour cream and some chopped green onions on mine.

"Okay, so we've got the big birthday party coming up," Alexis said, sprinkling some shredded cheese on her soup. She always likes to get right down to business. "Emma, what's the deal?"

"So, you guys know it's for Matt's and Sam's birthdays," Emma said. "All their friends are coming, so it's going to be really big."

"I keep forgetting. Why are they having their party together?" Katie asked.

"Even though they're a few years apart, their birthdays are only two days apart," Emma explained. "For a long time we had to have two separate parties, but this year Sam said it would be cool if they did it together, and Matt agreed."

"Sam's so nice," Katie said.

Emma rolled her eyes. "Listen, if you guys start drooling over my brothers, I am going to barf this delicious soup all over your table."

"Ewwww!" Katie, Alexis and I squealed. But I sort of can't blame Emma. Her little brother, Jake, is six, and he's totally adorable. Sam, the oldest, is in high school, and Katie and I both think he's superdreamy. Plus, he's amazingly nice, too. Then there's Matt, who's one grade above us. He's cute too, and Alexis has a crush on him, even though she swears she's over him.

"Before you barf, could you please tell me exactly how many people are going to be at this party?" Alexis asked.

Emma shrugged. "I'm not sure. Matt's inviting a bunch of guys from the basketball team, and Sam's swim team is coming. Plus our grandparents, I guess."

Alexis did some mental calculations. "So let's say forty people. Three dozen might not be enough, but four dozen might be perfect. Ask your mum, okay?"

"The way my brothers eat cupcakes, she'll probably want five dozen," Emma said.

"Hey, maybe we should do a sports theme," Katie suggested.

"I don't know," I said. "A sports theme seems kind of elementary school, doesn't it? Maybe there's a way to make it older. You know, sporty but suave."

Katie put down her spoon and looked at me. "Did you actually say 'sporty but suave'? What the heck does that mean?"

She started giggling, and Alexis and Emma joined in.

"You know, suave. Like, sophisticated," I said, but I was starting to giggle too. It did sound pretty silly.

"There is nothing suave about my brothers and their friends, trust me," Emma said.

"How about sporty but sweaty?" Katie suggested, and my friends collapsed into giggles again.

"Okay, okay!" I said. "But, seriously, hear me out. We don't want them to look like little kiddie cupcakes."

"Honestly, those boys won't care what they look like," Emma pointed out. "We could do a bunch of Plain Janes and they would be happy."

In the cupcake world, a Plain Jane is a vanilla cupcake with vanilla icing. They're very popular and very delicious, but not terribly exciting, either.

Alexis shook her head. "Every job we have is a business opportunity. We have to make our cupcakes stand out. There will be a lot of kids there, and if they remember our cupcakes, they might go home and tell their parents about them. We need to drum up more business."

"Definitely!" I agreed. "I need to make some extra money if I want that great pair of Kara Karen shoes I saw."

Now it was Katie's turn to roll her eyes. "Oh boy. Here she goes."

I took out my phone and called up my favourite picture of the shoes.

"Aren't they gorgeous?" I gushed, holding the phone out so Emma and Alexis could see.

"Ooh, they're pretty!" Emma agreed.

"Dylan would love those," said Alexis. Her older

35

sister is totally into fashion. "But they don't look very comfortable."

"That's exactly what I said!" Katie chimed in.

"Sometimes you have to sacrifice comfort for fashion," I told them, which is something my mum says. I sighed and put my phone away. I love my Cupcake Club friends, but they definitely do not care about fashion the way that I do. "Anyway, they're way expensive. I'm trying to save up for them, but it's going to take forever!"

"You know, I have a few more dogs than I can really handle this weekend," Emma said. Besides the Cupcake Club, she has her own dog-walking business. "Why don't you help me? I'll split the fee with you. It isn't much, but it will help."

"That would be great!" I replied, and then I remembered. "But I'm going to be with my dad all weekend."

"Maybe the weekend after that, then," Emma said.

"That would be very awesome," I said. I wished I could earn the money right then, but I guessed I would just have to wait a little longer for my shoes.

"So, we still need a plan for these cupcakes," Alexis prompted, bringing us back on track.

I pushed my empty soup bowl aside and took

out my sketchbook. I always have one on me.

"Give me a second," I said, and I closed my eyes and started envisioning what I thought the cupcakes should look like. In a few seconds my pencil was quickly moving over the paper.

"So, for the basketball team it's kind of obvious to decorate the round cupcakes to look like basketballs," I said. "But we don't have to go with orange icing and piped on laces. Maybe we could have a ball sticking on top of each cupcake."

"Ooh, we could make chocolate basketballs with a mold and use those," Katie suggested.

I picked up a blue pencil and kept sketching. "Then maybe for the swim team we could do blue icing and pipe waves onto it or something."

"I like how there's a different cupcake for each team," Alexis said.

Emma nodded. "My brothers will like that, because there's a special one for each of them."

"So what about flavours?" Alexis asked.

"Let me ask Matt and Sam what they want," Emma said.

Alexis looked satisfied. "Sounds like we have a plan."

"And it might not be suave, but I definitely think this is sporty chic," I said.

Katie shook her head. "Again, what does that even mean?"

I grinned. "It means that these cupcakes will be fabulous!"

"As always," Alexis added.

"So we're not doing sweaty cupcakes?" Katie asked, and we all started laughing again.

I love my Cupcake friends!

CHAPTER 6

I'm Not Sure What to Think

On Thursday morning I went to my locker before registration as usual to put in the books I didn't need and make sure I had the ones I did. And, as usual, Olivia was already there, looking in the mirror.

"Hi, Mia!" she said. "I just can't get this headband right. What do you think?"

She had on a blue headband, and as always, her hair looked perfect. There wasn't a strand out of place.

"Perfect!" I told her. Then I made a move to put my books in my locker.

But Olivia just turned back to the mirror. "How can you say that? I look terrible!" And then she started messing with her hair again.

"Well, the bell's going to ring soon," I told her.

"I know! It's so unfair. I can't go to class looking like this!" she wailed.

She had not taken my hint at all. I stood right next to her as she fussed some more. Then, finally, the bell rang.

I sighed. Now I'd have to rush to get to my locker between registration and first period. I hated doing that. But I guess I could understand. I know what it's like to have a bad hair day. Like, sometimes I swear I look like a monster, and Mum tells me I look beautiful.

Anyway, I couldn't wait until lunch because I had done some new, improved sketches of the basketball and swim-team cupcakes, and I was eager to show my friends. The morning crawled by and then, finally, it was lunchtime. I waited until we had finished eating so the drawings wouldn't get messed up, and then I took out my sketchbook.

"Hey, so last night I—" I began, but Olivia interrupted me.

"Oh my gosh, the funniest thing happened in maths class!" she said. "I totally forgot to tell you guys. You know Pat Delaney, right? So, Mr Rodriguez called her to the board and she took like, two steps and then she totally tripped on her shoelaces! And then she tried to stop herself from falling and she was, like, waving her arms all over the place. It was hilarious!"

"That doesn't sound hilarious to me," Katie said. "I like Pat. She's really cool."

"Was she hurt?" Emma asked.

Olivia shrugged. "I guess not. Anyway, it was just funny. She's, like, a total clutz."

"If you ever saw her play softball, you wouldn't say that," Alexis pointed out.

"Yeah," I joined in. "Pat is awesome. It's not cool to make fun of her like that."

Olivia held up both hands in protest. "Whoa, chill out! It's, like, classic comedy, right? You're *supposed* to laugh when someone falls down."

I saw Alexis shoot a look to Katie and Emma, a kind of raised-eyebrow look. At that moment, I started feeling bad for Olivia all over again. Maybe in her old school that kind of thing was funny.

I also noticed that when Katie and I took the bus, we never talked about Olivia, not since that first day. A couple of times I tried to bring Olivia up, but Katie would always change the subject. So after a while, I just stopped mentioning her.

"I can't believe you have to go to your dad's this

41

weekend," Katie said. "That movie about the polar bears is opening."

"I know," I answered. "But I promise I won't see it without you. Maybe we can go next week."

"Then I promise not to see it either," Katie said. "It'll be more fun if we go together."

That night, after football practice, homework, and dinner, I remembered I had volunteered to bring in the Friday cupcakes.

"Mum, what should I do? I totally forgot," I told her.

"I can help you," she said. "Anyway, you can make cupcakes in your sleep by now, can't you?"

I wanted to make something special for Olivia's first cupcake, but my best thing is decorating, so we went with chocolate cupcakes and chocolate icing. Then I rolled out some light blue fondant, which is this creamy sugar paste that you can sculpt, or roll out and cut shapes from it. When you see flowers on fancy wedding cakes, they're usually made of fondant.

Anyway, I've been trying to perfect my fondant flowers, and this was a good chance to practise. I cut the flattened fondant into circles and then rolled them up, so they looked like little roses. Then I cut out some tiny green leaves.

The finished cupcakes looked beautiful – shiny chocolate icing topped with perfect blue roses.

"Mia, they're beautiful!" Mum said when we had finished. "You are becoming such a professional!"

I hugged her. "I couldn't have done them without you. Thanks!"

When I got to school the next morning, Olivia was happy with her hair and her lip gloss, so I had plenty of time to get into my locker before registration. I had the cupcakes with me in a small plastic cupcake box, and I carefully placed it on top of my books.

After first period I realised that I had forgotten to take out my English notebook for second period, so I quickly ran to my locker. When I opened it up, I saw some of Olivia's books piled on my shelf again, on top of the cupcake box.

I shook my head. It's a good thing I hadn't used a cardboard box, or the cupcakes would have been ruined. I moved Olivia's books to the bottom shelf and then went to grab my English notebook – only it wasn't there.

"Oh, come on!" I said, frustrated. I *know* my notebook was in there. I had a feeling I knew what had happened – Olivia must have taken it by mistake.

43

I was about to be late for class, so there was nothing I could do but go to class without my notebook. Friday is the day that our teacher, Ms Harmeyer, checks to make sure we've written journal entries.

When I got to class, Ms Harmeyer told us to read chapter twelve in the novels we were working on and to pass up our notebooks. I hated not having something to pass up. After a few minutes, I heard her call out, "Ms Vélaz-Cruz. No notebook today?"

"Well, I'm sharing my locker with Olivia Allen, and I think she took it by mistake," I said.

The teacher shook her head. "You girls simply have to get more organised," she said in a frustrated voice, and I could feel myself blush. It wasn't fair! After all, I was just trying to help out one of my fellow classmates.

I didn't mention anything to Olivia during P. E. but I did bring it up at lunch, as soon as we sat down. Katie was the only other person at the table.

"Olivia, did you take my English notebook by mistake?" I asked. "It's a red composition book."

"Oh, that? Yeah, it looks just like my science book," she said. "Oops!"

"Well, maybe that's why we should keep our

books on separate shelves," I said, trying to be as tactful as possible. "Then this kind of thing wouldn't happen."

"Mmm hmm," Olivia said, but she wasn't even really listening to me. She was gazing over at the BFC table. "Wow, that is a great jacket Callie is wearing, isn't it?"

I am so easily distracted by fashion! I looked over and saw that Callie was wearing a really cool black jacket with no buttons and sort of puffy shoulders.

"Very cute," I agreed.

Emma and Alexis came to the table with trays of burgers and carrot sticks. Emma eyed the plastic cupcake box.

"Ooh, what did you make, Mia? I bet they're beautiful!" she said.

I opened the box and gently took out a cupcake.

"I'm practising my fondant flowers. What do you think?" I asked.

Olivia answered right away. "Oh my gosh, Mia, that is gorgeous!" she squealed. "You are, like, soooo talented! I bet you could go on one of those cupcake competition shows and win, like, a million pounds."

"Well, I couldn't go on without the Cupcake Club," I said. "We're a team."

"But I bet nobody but you can do flowers like these," Olivia gushed. "They're fabulous! You are probably the best cupcake maker in America – no, change that – the best cupcake maker in the entire world!" I blushed at the praise. I was pleased but also a little embarrassed.

"Do we want to talk about flavours?" Emma asked. "I got some suggestions from my brothers about the kind of cupcakes they like. Maybe we could go over them after we eat."

Alexis gave Emma a look again, and I saw Katie give kind of a nod.

"Actually, we all have a lot of studying to do right now," Alexis said. "We can do it at our next meeting."

Emma nodded without a word, and I was left feeling weird. I didn't know what to make of the secret looks my friends were giving one another. I felt kind of excluded. On the other hand, I wasn't really sure what to make of Olivia either. All this locker stuff was starting to get on my nerves.

Believe me, when your new friend *and* your old friends are starting to bug you, it doesn't feel good!

CHAPTER 7

Katie Vents

$\mathcal{K}$atie and I tell each other everything, so on the bus ride home, I told her about Olivia and the locker.

"And then I didn't have my English notebook for the lesson, and you should have seen the look that Ms Harmeyer gave me," I told Katie. "And the worst thing is, Olivia didn't even apologise to me."

"Mia, I'm so glad you said that!" Katie said. "I didn't want to say anything before, because I didn't know how you felt, but I just don't like Olivia. I really wish we didn't have to eat lunch with her."

I was surprised. Katie was always polite to Olivia, and I guess I'd always assumed that my friends liked Olivia, just like I did.

"Katie, I'm just a little annoyed with the locker

situation," I said. "But I really like Olivia."

Now it was Katie's turn to be surprised. "Oh, I thought you were just being nice to her because she's new. You mean you really like her? But she can be so mean!"

"What do you mean?" I asked.

"Like how she thought it was funny when Pat Delaney tripped," Katie said. "And Alexis has English with her, and she says Olivia makes rude comments about how everyone looks during most of the lesson. Well, except for Alexis. I think Olivia knows you won't be friends with her anymore if she does that."

I shook my head. "Honestly, Katie, I've never heard her do that. And as for Pat, I don't think that's such a big deal."

"So you seriously *like* her?" Katie asked. "I can't believe it!"

I started to get mad. "We have things in common. Besides, you've only known her for, like, a week. We need to give her a chance. When I first came here, it took a while before anybody even talked to me besides you and Alexis and Emma. What am I supposed to say? 'Sorry, but you can't eat with us anymore'? What's she supposed to do then? Sit all by herself?"

Katie held up both hands in protest. "Okay, okay, I get it. I don't want to hurt her feelings or anything," she said. "She can still sit with us if she wants to."

"Of course she wants to," I said.

"But I don't think she can be in the Cupcake Club," Katie said. "At least not now, anyway."

That sounded fair. "Fine," I said.

Secretly, I thought Katie was a little jealous. It really hurt her when Callie ditched her to join the Popular Girls Club. So I think she's worried that I'm going to do the same thing. Sometimes, when I go to the mall with Sophie and Lucy, these two girls I met last year who are pretty cool, Katie does this whole thing where she acts like it doesn't bother her, but I can tell it really does.

"You know, just because I'm friends with Olivia doesn't mean I'll stop being friends with you," I told her.

"I know," Katie said, but she sounded a little sad.

Then I started to sing this song I learned at summer camp. "Make new friends, but keep the old. One is silver and the other gold!"

Katie burst out laughing. "You are crazy," she told me, and then I knew that everything was okay between us.

Then the bus pulled up at the stop at the end of her road.

"Have a good weekend," I said.

Katie waved. "Yeah, have fun with your dad!"

A few stops later, I got off the bus, walked down the road and found Eddie waiting for me by the front door.

"Your mum's at a meeting, so I'm on train station duty," he informed me. "She said you packed last night."

I nodded. "My bag is upstairs. I just have to pick it up and get my toothbrush."

Since my parents divorced, I have become an expert in packing. If I bring too much stuff, my bag is too heavy to drag through the train station. But I also have to make sure I'm prepared for anything I do over the weekend, from hanging out outside to going to dinner in a nice restaurant. Once, my dad took me shopping, and I got a jacket and some clothes that I keep in my old bedroom, so that helps a lot.

Oh, and I also have to bring my school backpack, which can be extremely heavy. So my clothes suitcase is the kind that's on wheels, so I can pull it around. The hardest part is going up and down stairs with everything.

50

Eddie's really nice, and he helped me carry my stuff to the car and put it in the boot. I climbed into the passenger seat and then put on my seat belt, and we headed to the train station.

"So what's new and exciting?" Eddie asked.

"Not much," I said, but then I found myself launching into the whole Olivia story. "There's this new girl, Olivia, and we're sharing a locker because there isn't one for her. I like her, but the locker thing is getting kind of annoying. She takes forever looking in the mirror when I'm trying to get my stuff. And she's supposed to keep her stuff on the bottom shelf, but she puts it on the top shelf with mine, and it gets mixed up."

Eddie nodded. "You've got yourself a Carlos."

I was puzzled. "A Carlos?"

"Carlos Sanchez, my university roommate," Eddie explained. "He was a great guy, and we had a lot of fun together. But he was the worst roommate in the world. He would borrow my clothes, spill stuff on them and then stuff them back into my drawer. And he always ate my bologna and never replaced it."

"That is just rude," I agreed.

"It used to make me furious," Eddie said. "But the thing is, I still wanted to be his friend. So I just

51

pretended that Carlos the roommate was a different guy. And then I could hang out with Carlos the friend and enjoy myself."

Eddie's story was a little unusual, but I had to agree that it made sense. "So I guess I could do the same with Olivia," I said.

"Exactly," Eddie said. "Some people are just not meant to be in close quarters together. But that doesn't mean you can't be friends. In fact, why don't you invite her over for dinner one night next week? Your mum and I would like to meet her."

"Okay," I replied. I took out my phone and texted Olivia.

Off 2 my dad's. Do u want 2 have dinner at my house next week?

☺ Yes!!!!!!!!!!!!! Monday? Olivia texted back.

"Is Monday okay?" I asked Eddie.

"Sure," he replied. "I'm pretty sure your mum and I don't have anything scheduled."

Monday, I texted back. Ask ur mum if u can catch the bus home with me.

☺☺☺ Tx !!!!!!!! Olivia replied.

It made me feel good that she was so happy. In fact, I realised, I had made both Katie and Olivia happy in less than an hour. That's pretty good, don't you think?

CHAPTER 8

Sushi . . . and a Surprise

The train ride from Maple Grove to New York City takes more than an hour because of all the stops. It is extremely boring, so I always make sure I have music to listen to and a sketchbook. I know Katie feels sick if she reads or draws in a moving vehicle, but I am very lucky I don't have that problem. Otherwise, I would probably go insane. Insane on the train. I made a note to tell Katie about that one; she'd probably make up a funny song about it on the spot.

Dad was waiting for me when I got off the train at Penn Station. He always takes my luggage for me, so I don't have to lug it up the stairs. But first he gives me a superbig hug.

"*Mija*, you're getting taller every time I see

you!" he said. (Dad likes to call me "*mija*," which means "my daughter" in Spanish. It's pronounced "mee-ha," so it sounds a lot like my name.)

"Dad, I don't think I grew in two weeks," I protested.

"I think you did," Dad replied. "You are growing so fast!"

Then, like always, we piled into a cab and headed down to Tokyo 16, our favourite sushi restaurant. Besides having the most delicious sushi in the world, the place is beautiful on the inside: dark and calm, with a waterfall along the back wall. It's like you've been transported into another place.

We stuffed my bags against the wall and sat in our usual table by the waterfall. Our server, Yuki, brought us two steaming hot towels, so we could clean our hands. The towels smelled like flowers.

"Good to see you, Yuki," my dad said.

Yuki is in her twenties and wears her hair in a cute short haircut. She's very friendly.

"Will you and Mia be having the miso soup today?" she asked.

Dad looked at me, and I nodded. "*Mmm*, miso."

A few minutes later we were slurping on

steaming bowls of salty soup with green seaweed and tiny cubes of tofu floating in the broth.

"So, what's on our schedule this weekend, *mija*?" Dad asked.

"Well, I have to leave early Sunday, because of my football game," I said. "I hope that's okay."

"Of course," Dad said. "Your mum told me. I was thinking I could take the train out with you and see you play."

"Really?" I asked, and I felt really happy. Dad didn't used to like coming out to Maple Grove because he felt awkward being around Mum and Eddie. To be honest, it was a little awkward for me, too, to see my mum and dad in the same place, even though they're not together anymore. But I guess things were less awkward for them because he's been coming out more often for school events and stuff like that.

Dad misunderstood my response. "Only if you want me to."

"Definitely! Absolutely!" I told him. "I scored two goals last week."

Dad smiled. "That's my girl! I can't wait to see you play."

Then Yuki came and took our sushi order (spicy tuna roll and mango roll for me and a sashimi plate, which has thin slices of raw fish, for Dad). When Yuki left the table, my dad had a serious look on his face.

"*Mija*, I want to talk to you about something," he said.

Uh-oh, I thought. My dad hardly ever begins sentences like that. I flashed back to a year before, at this very table, when he told me he had a girl-friend named Alina. And she was just . . . well, awful!

So I must be psychic, because the next words out of his mouth were, "I have a new girlfriend."

"I knew it!" I cried, and I was probably pretty loud, because I noticed that people were looking at us. "Sorry," I whispered.

"It's okay," Dad said. "I know it didn't go so well last time. But Lynne isn't anything like Alina, I promise."

"I hope not," I said.

"And I think I made a big mistake the way I handled it last time," Dad admitted. "I didn't take your feelings into account. So this time, I'm going to ask you instead of telling you. Would you like to meet her sometime?"

I had to think it over. Sure, I like my stepdad, Eddie, but it took a long time to get used to him. I don't know if I could handle a stepmum, too.

But I knew Dad was going to date this Lynne person whether I wanted him to or not. And he was asking pretty nicely.

"Okay," I said hesitantly. "But maybe next visit? I need some time to get used to the idea."

Dad smiled. "Of course, *mija*. I have a feeling you will like her."

Yuki put our plates of food in front of us. I picked up a piece of spicy tuna roll with my chopsticks (I've been using them since I was three, so I'm pretty good) and dunked it in soy sauce.

"Mmm, umami," I said.

"Umami?" Dad asked.

"You know, like in the commercial," I said. "It's the way soy sauce tastes. It's like that extra-special flavour that makes everything taste better."

"Then you are my umami, Mia," Dad said. "You will always be my special girl, no matter who else I meet. That's how life is. We will both always be making new friends. But we'll always be important to each other. What's that saying? Make new friends, but keep the old. . ."

"One is silver and the other gold," I finished for him, and I felt all shivery. That's just what I said to Katie on the bus! Freaky, right? I wondered if this was a sign of some kind about Dad's girlfriend.

"So, what have we got planned for tomorrow?" Dad asked.

I grinned. "I'm meeting Ava, and we're going window shopping . . . *shoe* window shopping," I told him.

After dinner we just headed home for the night. We watched a little television, and then I went to sleep thinking about my wonderful shoes.

The next afternoon, me and my dad and my friend Ava were standing in front of the Kara Karen store. The shop had moved the heels – *my* heels – to the window.

"Your mum warned me about these," Dad said. "She said that under no circumstances am I to buy them for you. You're supposed to be earning half the money yourself."

I sighed. "I know, Dad," I said. "I just want to look at them, that's all."

Dad glanced across the street. "I'm going to grab a coffee. You girls have fun, okay?"

Ava and I stepped into the store. Ava Monroe is my first best friend, and she's gorgeous. She has shiny black hair and these beautiful brown eyes, and she's very petite, which helps make her graceful. We grew up together and played football on the same team for years.

"Wow, Mia, they're even more beautiful in person," Ava said (because, of course, I had already sent her the photo).

"They're the shoes of my dreams," I said with a sigh. "I knew you would understand."

As I lay in bed that night, my mind was jumbled with thoughts of silver and gold friends. Ava was my oldest friend, so she was gold. Then Katie was my next best friend, so that would make her silver (along with Alexis and Emma, of course). So what was Olivia? Bronze? That didn't seem right. Bronze didn't seem so nice; plus, I already told Katie that *she* was gold.

Maybe Ava was platinum, and Katie and Alexis and Emma were gold, and Olivia was silver. That felt better. Then I thought about what would happen when I made new friends *after* Olivia, and my thoughts got jumbled up again.

Maybe, I thought, as I drifted off to sleep, *it is just nice to have so many friends. Because all of them, in their own way, are supersparkly.*

CHAPTER 9

Olivia's Not-So-Sweet Side

When Katie and I got off the bus on Monday, Olivia was standing on the school steps waiting for me. She had a big grin on her face and looked superexcited.

"Mia, I can't wait to go to your house today!" she said, and she looked really excited. "It was soooo sweet of you to invite me."

I was glad that Olivia was so excited, but I was cringing inside, because Katie was right beside me. I probably should have mentioned my plans while Katie and I were on the bus, but I guess there was a part of me that was hoping she didn't have to know. I didn't want to hurt her feelings.

I glanced at Katie, and she looked okay, so I relaxed a little.

"Well, it was Eddie's idea," I said, partly for Katie to hear too. "He and my mum want to meet you."

"That is soooo sweet," Olivia repeated, and we all walked inside the school. Katie stopped at her locker, and Olivia and I headed farther down the hall to ours. When I opened the door, a bunch of crumpled papers fell out. I looked at Olivia.

She shrugged. "Oh, I dumped those in there on Friday. That's what lockers are for, right?"

No, that's what rubbish bins are for, I thought. But I didn't say it out loud. Olivia was just being a Carlos, and I was going to do what Eddie said and separate locker Olivia from everyday Olivia.

"Well, if you don't need them, maybe we could throw them out," I said cheerfully.

"I guess. There's a bin right over there," Olivia said, motioning with her head.

So I picked up the papers and threw them out while Olivia applied her lip gloss in the mirror. As I was walking back, my friends Sophie and Lucy walked by. One of the reasons I like them both is because they have their own unique senses of style. Sophie tends to dress sort of like a hippie, with big hoop earrings, peasant blouses and long skirts. Today, she was wearing a blue jumper over a tan billowy skirt and flats.

Sophie and Lucy said hi and kept going. When I got to my locker, I saw that Olivia was staring at them.

"What is up with that skirt?" she asked. "It looks like a tent. She could go camping in it!"

"Hey, Sophie is a friend of mine," I said. "And I like her look. I think she really pulls it off with her long curly hair and everything. Besides, I think her skirt is pretty."

Olivia shook her head. "Oh, come on, you wouldn't be caught dead in that!" she said and then started laughing.

"Well, just because I wouldn't wear it doesn't mean it doesn't look good on Sophie," I responded, hoping Olivia would understand. But she didn't.

"Well, if it rains today, we can all take shelter under her skirt," she said, cracking herself up again.

I was kind of upset with Olivia for saying that about Sophie, but I get that not everyone's idea about fashion is the same. Also, have you seen those TV shows where people talk about the fashions that celebrities wear? They say nasty things all the time, and everyone thinks it's funny.

At lunch that day, Olivia kept talking about how excited she was to go to my house. She was full of questions.

"What does your stepbrother look like? Is he cute? How many dogs do you have again? I can't wait to meet them!"

Katie got superquiet, and I could tell she was mad about the whole thing. But instead of feeling sorry for Katie, I felt kind of angry. I mean, I already told her I was going to be her friend, no matter what. Why couldn't she just trust me?

Katie and I always walk to social studies together after lunch, but not today. Olivia was distracting me with her questions, and when I looked up, Katie had already left without me.

"See you on the bus!" Olivia said happily, and then she ran off to class. As I walked out of the cafeteria, Alexis stopped me. I think she had been waiting for me by the door.

"Mia, are you cool with what Olivia was doing during lunch?" Alexis asked.

I was puzzled. "What do you mean?"

"The way she was bragging about going to your house, just to make Katie feel bad," Alexis said.

I shook my head. "She's just excited. She wasn't trying to hurt anybody."

Alexis made a face. "Did you not see her shooting looks at Katie the whole time?"

"She's not like that, honest," I said, although a

tiny part of me was beginning to wonder about that. "Just give her a chance."

Alexis glanced at her watch. "We'd better talk later, or we'll be late for class."

I was pretty distracted during social studies, thinking about what Alexis had said. I really didn't believe Olivia would hurt Katie on purpose like that. But then I remembered her mean comment about Sophie. Maybe locker Olivia wasn't the only one with problems.

I guess I'll find out later, I thought.

The bus ride home was a little awkward, because Olivia was riding the bus with me and Katie. But I wasn't about to make Katie angry by leaving our usual seat, so when Olivia came on, I just kind of shrugged, and Olivia found a seat in the back. I turned to Katie and said, "I know you don't like Olivia, but I really think the more you get to know her, you'll change your mind. She can be really fun."

Katie sighed and then said, "I don't think so, but I hope I change my mind, I really do – I don't like disagreeing with you about anything, and especially about friends. So let's talk about something else – I'd rather talk about *anything* instead of Olivia – even shoes!" We both laughed, and

I changed the subject. Katie and I chatted away until she got off the bus, and then Olivia joined me. Soon we got to my stop.

"Ooh, your house is so pretty!" Olivia said as we walked up to it.

I have to admit the house is one of the nicest things about living in the suburbs. It was Eddie and Dan's house before my mum and I moved in. It's a white two-story house with a porch in the front and a big lawn that Dan hates to mow.

"Thanks," I said.

When I opened the door, my two little white Maltese, Tiki and Milkshake, came to greet us. Tiki always pats his little paws on my ankles, and Milkshake does a happy dance and wags her tail.

"Awww, they're soooo cute!" Olivia said, and she knelt down to pet them. "I have a Chihuahua at home. Maybe they could be friends."

Then my mum came out of the kitchen. "You must be Olivia," she said. "Nice to meet you."

"Nice to meet you too, Mrs Vélaz-Cruz," Olivia said.

Mum smiled. "Actually, it's Mrs Valdes now. Confusing, isn't it? It's been nearly a year, but I'm still getting used to it myself."

Then she nodded towards the dining room.

"I've set up a snack in there for you, so you can do your homework before dinner."

"Thanks, Mum," I said, and I motioned for Olivia to follow me. She was frowning.

"Homework?" she asked. "I thought we could, you know, see your room and stuff."

"Yeah, well, my mum's pretty strict about that," I said. "Homework first, fun later."

Mum had put out some yogurt cups, fruit and a pitcher of iced tea for us. I grabbed a mango yogurt and sat back. "We can eat first," I told Olivia.

Olivia took a strawberry yogurt. "So, I was wondering about those girls in the BFC," she said. It was the first time she had mentioned them to me. "You know, Callie, Maggie and Bella. So what's their deal?"

"Well, last year they were led by this girl, Sydney, but she moved to California," I said. "They used to be called the Popular Girls Club. Sydney was kind of mean and didn't let anybody join except for Callie. Now I guess Callie's kind of in charge. They let girls sit with them sometimes, but I don't think they have any new members yet. They're kind of exclusive."

"What about you?" Olivia asked.

"What do you mean?" I replied.

"Well, you're like the most stylish girl in the whole school," Olivia said. "So why aren't you one of them?"

"Actually, Sydney asked me to join," I admitted. "But I didn't want to. I'd rather stay with my real friends in the Cupcake Club."

Olivia looked impressed. "You know, I don't understand why the BFC are so high-and-mighty. Maggie's hair looks like she stuck her finger in a socket. Doesn't she know she can buy products to fix it?"

"Hey, I thought you were friendly with her!" I said. "Don't say mean things about her. And, anyway, Maggie's not so bad."

"I wasn't being mean," Olivia protested. "I just said her hair is horrible. That's constructive criticism. If you're trying to be popular, you should have good hair, right?"

I was starting to feel uncomfortable. This was the second time today I had heard Olivia's "constructive criticism," but it sounded just plain mean to me.

"It's just the way you said it," I told her.

Then Olivia's eyes got teary. "Oh, Mia, come on. Don't be like that. I have no one but you to really talk to at school. Don't be mad."

"I'm not mad," I said slowly. And I wasn't, exactly. But I was starting to think that everyday Olivia was just as bad as locker Olivia, and I wasn't sure what to do about that.

"You must know how it feels, because you were new," Olivia said. "Half of the girls won't even talk to me. If it wasn't for you, I'd be a total loser."

And with that, she got me. I felt like I owed it to her to be her friend.

"Hey, I can't believe I haven't showed you these yet," I said, changing the subject as I reached for my phone. I held up the screen so she could see. "My dream shoes. I found them in the Kara Karen boutique in SoHo. What do you think?"

"Oh my gosh, they're fabulous!" she said, practically screaming. "They're the greatest shoes I've ever seen in my entire life!"

"I know!" I replied.

Then we heard my mum's voice coming from the kitchen.

"Girls? Are you doing homework in there?"

"Of course, Mum!" I replied, and then Olivia and I burst into giggles.

CHAPTER 10

Trying to Find the Right Mix

The rest of my day with Olivia was really fun. We did our homework, and Mum made Caesar salad, fish, and rice for dinner, and Olivia had funny stories to tell about her Chihuahua, and everyone seemed to like her.

Then, while Olivia and I were waiting for her dad to pick her up, Olivia asked me something.

"So, you know, I was wondering," she said. "You were saying how exclusive the BFC is. Is the Cupcake Club exclusive too?"

It was an awkward question. We always got down on the BFC for not inviting new members, but we had never invited anybody to join the Cupcake Club either.

I replied with Alexis's standard answer.

"Well, it's more than a club, it's a business," I said. "So we keep it small, you know? So we can actually make a profit."

"Oh, well, I was just wondering, that's all," Olivia said. "I mean, it sounds like fun."

She wasn't asking outright to join the club, but it was a pretty big hint. And I kind of felt like she had a point. If we were a club, we should be open to everybody. Maybe there was a way to separate the club part from the business part somehow.

I knew I was going to have to talk to the Cupcake Club about this, and I kind of dreaded it. I had already promised Katie that Olivia wouldn't be in the club. And now I was kind of going back on it.

I had my chance to bring it up the next night at our Cupcake Club meeting. After school we all walked to Alexis's house. She and Emma live on the same road, and it's close to the school, so we don't have to take the bus. We gathered around Alexis's spotless kitchen table, and she took out her laptop.

"So, everyone agrees on Mia's designs for the cupcakes?" Alexis asked, and we all nodded. "Before I can make up a shopping list, we need to decide on flavours. Emma, what did your brothers say?"

"Well, Matt loves peanut butter and jam more

than anything, so he was wondering if we could do a P-B-and-J cupcake," Emma said. "Katie, I remembered that your mum made you one for the first day of middle school."

Katie nodded. "They're pretty easy. You make a vanilla cupcake, and then you put grape jam into an injector thingie and squirt some into each cupcake. Then you top it off with peanut-butter-and-cinnamon frosting."

"The little basketball will look cute sticking out of the peanut butter icing," I said. "The colours will work together."

Alexis started typing. "So besides our usual ingredients, we will need grape jam, peanut butter and . . ."

"Cream cheese," Katie said. "I'm pretty sure the peanut-butter icing is made with cream cheese. Oh, and we already have the cupcake injector, so we don't need that."

"Cream cheese," Alexis said aloud as she typed, and then she looked at Emma. "Okay, what about Sam?"

"Sam said that everything we make is delicious, so he doesn't care," Emma said.

"That is so sweet!" Katie said.

"He is the best," I added.

Emma made a face. "You should smell his trainers after he goes running," she said. "Anyway, we still need to pick a flavour."

"I am dying to try out my new cupcake plunger," Katie said. "Maybe we could do, like, pudding-filled cupcakes or something."

"Mmm, pudding cupcake," Alexis said. "So, like, a vanilla cupcake with chocolate pudding?"

"Vanilla pudding would go better with the blue icing," I pointed out.

"But the pudding will be *inside* the cupcake," Alexis argued.

"Yes, but when you bite into it, you'll see the pudding," I said.

Alexis nodded. "Good point. Okay, then. We need some boxes of vanilla pudding. I like this. A cupcake with a surprise inside will get people talking. It's good for business."

"It's kind of a lot of work, though," Emma said. "I mean, we're doing six dozen cupcakes, and both of them have extra stuff inside them."

I figured this was my chance to jump in.

"Maybe we just need some extra help," I said casually.

Alexis narrowed her eyes suspiciously. "What do you mean?"

73

"Like, maybe, once in a while, we could invite people to help us," I said. "People who are interested in being part of the Cupcake Club. We wouldn't have to split the profits with them or anything."

"You mean people like Olivia," Alexis said flatly.

"Well, yes," I said. "I mean, she pointed out that the Cupcake Club seems kind of exclusive, and we don't want to be like the BFC, do we?"

"Of course not," Emma spoke up. "It's just . . ."

"Olivia likes *you*, but she hardly ever talks to us or tries to be nice to us," Katie blurted out.

"Katie's right," Alexis agreed. "When we're in lunch, she's always looking around the room, like she's scoping out someone better to talk to. It's like we're not good enough for her or something."

"And she is such a flirt!" Emma jumped in. "Anytime a guy comes near her, she turns into a whole different person."

"What does that have to do with making cupcakes?" I asked.

There was an awkward pause for a mument. Alexis and Emma and Katie looked at one another. Finally, Katie spoke up.

"I think Mia has a good point," she said. "We don't want to be exclusive, like the BFC. But, remember, we're not just a club. We're a business, too."

"So, maybe we can keep the business separate," I said. "Businesses hire people, don't they? Maybe we could hire Olivia to help us with the cupcakes."

"But then we'd each make less money," Emma said. "Oh, and that reminds me. I have an extra dog-walking client on Saturday. Can you come help me after practice? Like I said, I'll split my fee with you!"

"I should be done by eleven," I said. "Is that okay? I would love to help. I still don't have enough money for my shoes."

"Which is another reason why we shouldn't hire Olivia to help with the cupcakes," Alexis said.

"Okay, you win!" I said. "But maybe there's something else we could let her do where we don't have to pay her. Let's just think about it, okay?"

Alexis shrugged. "Sure. Now let's get back to our shopping list."

And just like that, we were back to business again, which was okay with me. Even though Olivia wasn't part of the club, at least my friends weren't mad at me. I could never stay mad at my Cupcake girls!

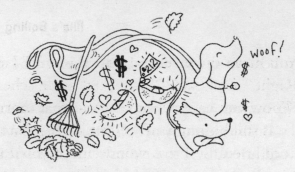

CHAPTER 11

How Could You Forget a Whole Kid?

On Wednesday night I Skyped with my dad. He gave me a laptop with a webcam, just so we could see each other on the days he doesn't have me. I have to admit that it's kind of nice to see his face instead of just talking on the phone.

"*Hola, mija.* How's it going?" Dad asked after his face popped up on the screen.

"Good," I replied. Sometimes I don't really know what to say with him. "I got an A on my Spanish quiz."

"Good job, *mija*!" Dad congratulated me. "I'm so proud of you."

"Thanks," I said.

"So, I wanted to talk with you about the next weekend I have with you," Dad said.

"You mean the weekend after this one," I said.

"Right," Dad said. "I checked your schedule, and I know you have a football game that morning. But I was still hoping you'll come out on Saturday afternoon. Because I was wondering if you'd want to go to the Museum of Natural History with me and Lynne and Ethan on Sunday."

I was puzzled. "Ethan? Who's Ethan?"

"Remember, I told you," Dad replied. "Ethan is Lynne's son. He's five years old."

"Um, no, you definitely did *not* tell me," I said.

"I'm sure I did," Dad protested.

"Well, I think I would have remembered that," I said. "Seriously, how could you forget to tell me about a kid?"

I could see that Dad was getting a little frustrated with me. "Well, I'm telling you now. He's a sweet little boy. So how about the Museum of Natural History?"

Now, my favourite museum in New York is the Metropolitan Museum of Art, because there are these awesome costume exhibits. I had a feeling that five-year-old Ethan probably didn't want to look at costumes and that's why we were going to the natural history museum. I haven't been there since I was about five.

I could have complained, but Dad seemed so happy about it all, and at least he was asking me, right? So I decided to be mature about it.

"Sure, Dad," I said. "We can go to the museum."

Dad was practically beaming with happiness. "We will have fun, I promise. I can't wait, *mija*."

"Okay, Dad. Love you," I said.

"Love you, too!" And then we signed off.

Mum walked by my bedroom door. "Talking to your dad?" she asked.

"He was asking about next weekend, if I can come after my football game," I said. "I told him okay." I left out the part about going to the museum with his new girlfriend and her son, because I didn't want her to feel weird.

Mum nodded.

"Oh, and I forgot to tell you, I'm going to help Emma walk dogs this Saturday after my game," I said. "For the shoes, of course."

"Good for you," Mum said. "And Eddie and I were talking. If you want to rake some leaves this weekend, we'll pay you."

Inside, I groaned. I hate raking leaves. But I love shoes more, so I answered her happily.

"I'll do it!" I replied. "I will be the best leaf raker in all of Maple Grove."

✿

So Saturday, after my early football game, I began Operation Save for Shoes. Mum dropped me off at Emma's house, so that I could help her with the dogs.

Emma was outside waiting for me.

"I'm so glad you can help," she said. "I have this new client, Mrs Oliver, who has two dogs, and she's watching her sister's dogs while her sister is away, and it's hard for me to walk four at the same time."

"It'll be fun," I said. "I walk Tiki and Milkshake all the time."

Then Emma handed me some brown plastic bags. "For . . . you know, clean up."

I nodded. I was pretty used to cleaning up after my Maltese.

"We can walk there," Emma said. "She lives over on Thompson Street."

As we were about to leave, Emma's little brother, Jake, ran up. His blond hair was all messy and he looked adorable, as always.

"Emma, I want to come! I can help!" Jake said.

"Jake, I already told you, Mrs Oliver's dogs are too big for you," Emma said. "Go back inside. Dad's watching you this morning."

Jake's blue eyes got wide. "Emma, pleeeeease?"

He looked cuter than any kitten video you've ever seen on the Internet. I don't know how Emma resisted him, but she was pretty firm.

"Inside, Jake."

Jake frowned, but he listened to Emma and ran right inside.

"Thank goodness," Emma said. "He can be so annoying!"

Listening to Emma made me think of that kid Ethan. If my dad and Lynne got serious, that would make Ethan my little brother.

"Seriously, Emma," I said as we walked. "I know you said that Jake is annoying, but we all think Jake is so cute. Is it really that bad having a little brother?"

Emma looked thoughtful. "Well, most of the time it's okay. But he can be annoying a lot. Like, I never have any privacy because he's always bugging me. But then sometimes I look at his face and just want to hug him, you know?"

I nodded. "It's just . . . my dad wants me to meet his new girlfriend, and she has this five-year-old kid, and it's freaking me out a little bit," I admitted. "I was an only child for a long time. Then I had to get used to having an older brother. I'm not sure I could handle having a little brother, too."

"I think about being an only child sometimes,"

Emma confessed. "But then I think I would miss my brothers sometimes. Even Matt."

"Well, maybe Ethan will be as adorable as Jake," I said. "That wouldn't be so bad."

"Besides, your dad just started dating this woman, right? So it's not like it's serious," Emma said.

I thought about the way my dad's face lit up when he talked about Lynne, and I wasn't so sure.

We stopped in front of a small grey house, and Emma used a key to open up the back door.

"Stand behind me," Emma warned.

I did as I was told, and just in time, because four huge, slobbering yellow dogs bounded to the door and pounced on Emma. She's shorter than I am, so I was surprised they didn't knock her down. With her blonde hair and blue eyes and pretty dresses, Emma doesn't exactly look tough, but she's one of the toughest people I know.

"Sit!" Emma commanded, and all four dogs sat at once, gazing at her expectantly. Emma took four leashes off a hook on the wall.

"I'll leash them up, then you can take Goldie and Tigger," she told me.

"Which ones are those?" I asked, because all the dogs looked pretty much the same.

81

"I'll give them to you," Emma said, and soon I was holding on to leashes with a giant dog at each end. I was pretty sure they both weighed a lot more than I did.

Emma is a real pro, because she led the way as we walked the dogs down the street, and all four dogs followed her, like furry soldiers. Goldie and Tigger didn't even pull or strain, and I was glad, because walking two tiny Maltese had not prepared me for this.

When the walk was over, we brought the dogs back to Mrs Oliver's house and Emma took an envelope from the kitchen table before we left and locked up. She handed me fifteen dollars.

"Here's your half," she said. "Any time you want to help out, just let me know."

"Thanks!" I said.

When I got home, my arms were already aching, but Eddie greeted me with a big smile – and a rake.

"Can I please eat lunch first?" I moaned before he even said a word.

"Why not? The leaves aren't going anywhere," Eddie joked.

So after I ate a cheese sandwich I raked . . . and raked . . . and raked for hours. I mean, literally, hours. I'm not exaggerating. My body hurt all over and I was exhausted, but I didn't care, because Eddie gave me twenty bucks. I didn't need much more to get the shoes. In fact, I'd probably have enough money after we got paid for Matt and Sam's party.

That night, I stretched out on my bed and gazed at the sketch of the shoes I had drawn.

"Soon, soon, you will be mine," I whispered, and then I laughed because I realised I sounded like a creepy movie villain or something. But I couldn't help it. I couldn't wait to get those shoes!

CHAPTER 12

My First Design Client

The next morning I woke up to the sound of my phone beeping. My CC friends know to never text me before nine a.m. on a weekend. Maybe it was Dad? He knew better than that too.

Groaning, I reached for the phone and looked at the screen through blurry eyes. It was from Olivia.

Want 2 hang out this afternoon?

I had to think for a minute. I still had an essay to write for English, but that wouldn't take long. Mum hadn't said anything about plans for today. And I definitely didn't feel like raking more leaves.

Sure. What do u want 2 do? I typed.

Let's hang at ur house, Olivia replied.

That sounded okay with me.

C u at 1, I typed.

TTYL!!!! ☺☺, she responded immediately.

Then I rolled over and went back to sleep. When I went downstairs later, Dan was sitting at the kitchen table eating a plate of eggs, bacon and toast.

"You must have been tired, Mia," Mum told me as she walked into the kitchen. "You even slept later than Dan."

"Hey, I don't sleep late," Dan protested.

"Do you want some eggs?" Mum asked me.

"I'll just eat some cereal," I said, reaching for the cabinet. "Oh yeah, and is it okay if Olivia comes over for a while? Like, at one?"

"Just as long as it's okay with her parents," Mum replied.

I got a bowl, a box of cereal and some milk from the fridge and started to get my cereal ready, still yawning. Then I heard my phone beep in my pocket. Another text.

I took out my phone and saw that this text was from Katie.

Want 2 see the polar bear movie today?

"Oh no," I said out loud, and Dan looked at me quizzically.

I remembered talking to Katie about seeing the movie, but I don't think we had set a date. I really wanted to go, but it would be rude to cancel on Olivia.

I also thought about making some excuse to Katie, but then I realised Olivia would probably talk about it at lunch tomorrow. There was no easy way out of this.

Can't. Olivia coming over. Maybe 2 nite? I cringed as I typed those words.

Can't go 2 nite. Mum and I are going 2 her friend's for dinner, Katie wrote back.

I wasn't sure what to say, so I went with a frowny face.

☹

I might go see the movie anyway, Katie texted me. Hope that's ok.

What could I say? I really wanted to see it with her, but I couldn't tell her to wait. That wouldn't be fair.

K! I typed. Txt me a review when it's over.

K, Katie typed back, and that was the end of our conversation.

I couldn't tell if she was mad or not.

But there was no point in worrying about it, right? I wasn't going to have a miserable afternoon just because I might have upset Katie. And when Olivia came over, we had a great time.

"We need to spend some time in your closet," Olivia said when she arrived. "Last time was too much homework, not enough clothes!"

"What are we waiting for?" I asked, and we headed upstairs.

I used to kind of hate my bedroom. When I first moved in, it had old-lady wallpaper and old furniture that didn't match, but Eddie helped me totally redo it. He took down the wallpaper (which was the really hard part), and after changing my mind, like, a thousand times, we painted the walls in this pale turquoise colour, and then we painted the furniture gleaming white, with black around the trim and stuff, and it looks totally cool. Plus, I have a really big closet, which is almost as big as my whole bedroom in my dad's apartment in Manhattan.

"Oh my gosh, Mia, this closet is ah-may-zing!" Olivia cried as she opened up the door. "You have the most fabulous clothes!"

"I get a lot of them for free," I explained. "From my mum's clients."

"It is sooo cool that your mum has a fashion career," Olivia said. "My mum sells mattresses. Boooring!"

She pulled out a white sleeveless dress with black polka dots that I got this spring.

"Ooh, this is adorable! Can I try it on?"

"Of course," I said. When I'm in Manhattan, Ava and I are always trying on each other's clothes. I miss having someone to do that with here.

The afternoon went by pretty quickly. Since winter is coming up, I've been trying to figure out how to style my winter outfits, and Olivia's mad layering skills came to the rescue. We came up with seven new outfits just based on what was in my closet. And Olivia didn't say anything mean about anybody – not once.

Right after Olivia left at four o'clock I got a few texts from Katie.

Baby bear cute.
Baby bear gets lost.
Baby bear finds mum.
The end. ☺

So it looked like everything was okay with Katie after all, and I was really relieved.

I got more good news the next morning at school. I was walking to my and Olivia's locker when Olivia came out of the principal's office and headed towards me.

"Hey, so this kid Michael Hanna moved or something and I can have his locker," she told me. "It's right around the corner from yours."

She held up a note. "Principal LaCosta gave us a note so we can skip registration and move the stuff to my new locker."

"That's great!" I said, but Olivia didn't look exactly happy.

"It's fun sharing a locker with you," she said. "I'll miss you."

"I'll miss you, too," I said, but I was kind of lying. Because inside I was thinking, *Hooray! No more locker Olivia!*

We went to my locker and each grabbed a handful of Olivia's stuff and brought it to her new locker. Olivia opened it up and turned to me.

"Would you mind bringing the rest? I'll start getting it organised," she said.

"Um, sure," I said. I made a couple more trips with Olivia's books and makeup, and on the last trip, I took the mirror off the door, cringing as it tore my wallpaper. I'd have to find something to put there to cover it up.

When I handed Olivia the mirror, she gave a big sigh.

"My locker is sooo boring!" she complained. "I wish I could make it look cool like yours."

"Of course you can," I said. "You have an awesome sense of style."

"Not like *yours*," Olivia said. "I could never be as good as you, Mia. You're practically a professional!"

"Maybe I should go into business," I joked. "Mia's Locker Makeovers."

But Olivia took me seriously. "You could make over my locker! I would love that. I could be, like, your first client."

I thought about it. Designing my locker was a lot of fun. It would be fun to decorate Olivia's, too.

"Okay," I said. "Let's talk more at lunch."

So at lunchtime, Katie was telling me about the polar bear movie when Olivia interrupted us.

"So, Mia," she said, "I was thinking of how we can decorate my locker. Maybe turquoise and black, like your room. Or maybe animal prints. Or both! What do you think?"

I took out my sketchbook.

"Animal-print wallpaper could be cute," I said, sketching it out as I talked. "And you need a cool mirror, of course. Maybe that could be the focal point. Oh, and extra shelves for your makeup!"

I could see Alexis roll her eyes across the table, but I didn't care. I was having fun.

"That all looks ah-may-zing!" Olivia said. "How soon can we do it?"

I thought about how my mum handled her clients. "Let me come up with some sketches for you, and a budget. Maybe by Friday, okay?"

Olivia pouted. "Friday? That's forever!"

But I wanted to do the job right. I kind of liked the idea that Olivia was my first client. I wasn't going to charge her, of course, but I still wanted to do things professionally.

"I'll definitely have it by Friday, I promise," I assured her.

So when I wasn't doing homework or having football practice, I worked on sketches for Olivia's locker. I found samples of wallpaper and mirrors and shelves online and printed them out. By Friday, I had a whole presentation for Olivia. We looked at it while we ate the lemon cupcakes Alexis had made.

"Ooh, this mirror is perfect!" Olivia said, pointing to one I had printed out. "And I love the wallpaper and the shelves and the makeup light. Soooo cool!"

I did some quick adding. "The stuff all comes to about forty dollars. You can get all of it at the stores in the mall. You can keep the proposal, so you know what to look for."

"Wow, that's all so complicated," Olivia said. "I probably wouldn't even get the right stuff. Would you mind doing it, and I'll pay you back?"

Once again, I saw Alexis roll her eyes, but Olivia wasn't asking anything outrageous. Mum did this kind of thing for her clients all the time. She did the shopping, and then she sent them a bill, and they paid her.

"No problem," I said. I could use my shoe savings to get the stuff over the weekend, and then I'd have the money back on Monday. "This is going to be so fabulous. Even more fabulous than my locker!"

"I hope so," Olivia said.

For a second, I wondered, did she just mean that she hoped her locker was fabulous? Or did she hope that hers looked better than mine? But then I felt silly thinking that. Mostly, I was superexcited to be doing the locker design. And I really liked knowing that Olivia admired my sense of style. She was turning out to be a really nice friend.

CHAPTER 13

The Monster at the Museum

Saturday was a pretty hectic day, because after my football game, I had to shower and change so I could make the one thirty train to Manhattan. It's always weird when I have to go in on Saturday because Dad and I don't have our usual sushi routine. But this time I had a plan: Dad was bringing Ava with him, and we were going to go shopping for Olivia's locker stuff in midtown, which is crowded and filled with all kinds of shops.

Ava ran up to me and gave me a big hug as soon as I got off the train.

"Mum says I can have dinner with you guys," she told me. "Yay!"

"I'm kind of in the mood for Italian," I said. "When it starts to get chilly out, I crave pasta."

"How about the Ravioli Hut?" Ava suggested. "They have forty-six different kinds of ravioli!"

I looked at Dad, and he shrugged. "Whatever you girls want. But you need to do some shopping first, right?"

The shops I needed were close to the train station, so we walked. Because it was Saturday afternoon, the streets were crowded with tourists. Dad walked right behind me and Ava, so he wouldn't lose us.

After about ten blocks we reached Dazzle, an accessories shop. They had the mirror I wanted, along with racks and racks of other amazing stuff, like jewellery, scarves and hats. Dad went to get coffee, like he always does when he takes us shopping, and Ava and I walked around the shop.

Ava picked up two long, dangly earrings with keys hanging from them. They reminded me of Olivia's necklace. She held them up to her ears.

"What do you think?" she asked.

"Adorable!" I replied. "I think keys must be a big thing this year. Olivia has a necklace that would match those perfectly."

"So what are we getting for Olivia again?" Ava asked.

"I'm designing her locker." I reached into my

bag and took out the proposal I had created for Olivia. "I did a bunch of sketches and printed out samples of stuff, and she picked what she wanted. I'm going to buy it for her, and she'll pay me back."

"I thought you were saving for those shoes?" Ava asked.

"I know, but I don't have exactly enough yet, and anyway, Olivia will pay me on Monday," I replied.

"Wow, you're being totally professional," Ava told me, and the compliment meant a lot. That's what I was trying to do.

I bought the perfect mirror, just the right size and with this really pretty border with lots of bling on it. Then we headed to the Organiser Store two blocks down to get a special light that we could stick above the mirror so Olivia could see better when she put on her lip gloss. We got some small shelves there too.

"This is going to be an awesome locker," Ava said. "Olivia is lucky. Hey, I forgot to ask you. Did you see that polar bear movie yet?"

I shook my head. "I was supposed to go with Katie, but . . . well, Olivia came over."

"Wow, you're spending a lot of time with

Olivia," Ava remarked. "How does Katie feel about that?"

"I think she's a little bit hurt," I admitted. "But it's not fair. I'm still her friend. She's just sensitive, that's all."

"I'm just saying, you've been talking about Olivia a lot lately," Ava said.

I didn't get mad when Ava said that, because she's outside the situation, if you know what I mean. Since I moved to Maple Grove, she's always given me good advice about what happens there. So it got me thinking – maybe I was ignoring Katie a little bit. And that wasn't cool.

So that night, after we finished shopping, stuffed ourselves with spinach and cheese ravioli and took Ava home, I stretched out on my bed and texted Katie.

Miss u. Want 2 hang out Monday?

Science report due Tuesday. ☹, Katie texted back right away.

Me too! Let's do it together! My house? I wrote.

K! ☺, Katie wrote back.

I have to admit I was feeling pretty good about things. Katie was happy, Olivia was happy, and I was close to getting my dream shoes. I went to sleep with a smile on my face.

And then on Sunday, my good mood was totally destroyed.

Dad arranged for us to meet Lynne and Ethan at the museum. It's a huge, beautiful building with big stone steps and it's right across from Central Park. The steps were pretty crowded, so I looked around to see if I could guess who Lynne and Ethan might be. Then Dad pointed to a woman at the top step.

"Hello!" he called out, waving, and Lynne waved back.

She was wearing a plaid peacoat, a denim skirt and knee-high black boots. Her hair kind of reminded me of Katie's – light brown and wavy. I didn't see what Ethan looked like right away because he was hiding behind his mum.

Lynne smiled as we walked up. "Mia, I'm so glad to meet you! Your dad has told me so much about you," she said.

"Thanks," I said. "It's nice to meet you too."

"And this is Ethan," Lynne said, reaching for his arm. But Ethan just grabbed on to her leg and held on.

I sort of knelt down and said in my friendliest voice, "Hi, Ethan. I'm Mia."

Ethan stuck his head out, and I saw a head of messy brown hair, blue eyes and a runny nose.

"Go away!" he yelled, and then he ducked behind his mum again.

"I'm sorry," Lynne said. "Ethan is getting over a cold, and he didn't sleep well last night."

Dad looked behind Lynne. "Sorry you're feeling bad, little guy," he said, but Ethan didn't respond. Then Dad looked at Lynne and me and gave us a big smile. "What do you say we explore this museum?"

We followed Dad inside, and he paid for our admission.

"Can we look at the blue whale first?" I asked.

The blue whale is probably the most famous thing in the whole museum. It's a life-size model of a blue whale, the largest animal on Earth. It hangs from the ceiling and you can walk underneath it. It's totally incredible. Besides, I know Katie loves it, and I wanted to take a picture to send her.

"I want to see the dinosaurs!" Ethan yelled.

"We'll see the dinosaurs," Lynne said patiently. "But first we're going to see the whale."

"But I don't *like* the whale!" he said, stomping his foot.

"That's okay," I said. "We don't have to see the whale."

"No, it's all right," Lynne insisted. "Ethan has to learn to be patient."

So we walked to the big room where the whale is, and before we could even walk through the door, Ethan ran away like a rocket.

"Ethan!" Lynne cried, panicked.

"I'll get him," my dad volunteered.

Let me tell you, this kid was fast. Dad goes to the gym almost every day, but he had a hard time catching up with him. Then when he did catch up to him, you could hear Ethan screaming.

Lynne and I looked at each other.

"We'd better find them," Lynne said apologetically.

We followed the sound of the screaming to the dinosaur wing. Dad was holding Ethan's hand, but the kid was just yelling and yelling and people were staring. He ran to Lynne as soon as he saw us.

"Mummy! Mummy! I want to see the dinosaurs!" he wailed.

"It's fine," I insisted. "Let's see the dinosaurs."

Lynne and my dad gave in because we all stayed to see the dinosaurs. Ethan raced around and asked a million questions about each one. Finally, Ethan said he was hungry, and we went to the snack shop in the museum. It was packed, but we managed to find a table. My dad asked what we wanted, and then he got on line to get the food for us.

"I'll help," I offered.

"Don't worry, sit and relax," Dad said. "I want you guys to get to know one another."

I reluctantly sat down and Lynne smiled at me. "So, Mia, how do you like school this year?"

"Well, a lot better than I did before," I said, but before I could explain why, Ethan started whining and complaining about how hungry he was and asking if he could go back to see the dinosaurs. So Lynne and I couldn't have much of a conversation.

Finally, Dad came back with a tray of food. He put an order of chicken fingers in front of Ethan, along with a carton of apple juice.

Ethan picked up the juice and frowned.

"I wanted orange juice!" he yelled, and he slammed down the carton so hard that the cardboard container split and juice spilled all over the table.

"I'll get it!" Dad cried, and he jumped up and ran to get some napkins.

I was totally appalled. This kid was a monster! I imagined having to be his big sister and shuddered.

CHAPTER 14

Thank Goodness for Katie

Dad didn't have much to say after the museum disaster, and I could tell that he was embarrassed and disappointed. I couldn't think of anything comforting to say to him, because all I could think about was how terrible it would be to live with Ethan.

The next morning, I told Katie the whole story on the bus, and she was very sympathetic. Then we said good-bye and headed to registration, where I handed Olivia a bag with all of her locker supplies.

"Oh my gosh, Mia, thank you, these are soooo awesome!" she squealed as she looked through the bag.

I handed her the receipts. "It came to forty-one dollars and thirty-six cents," I said.

Olivia absently took them from me. "Mmm

hmm," she said, and she tucked them into her notebook. She didn't say anything about paying me back.

"So you would not believe what happened to me yesterday," I said. "Remember I told you my dad wanted me to meet his girlfriend and her kid? Well, we went to the museum and—"

"So when are you going to put all the stuff up?" Olivia asked, interrupting me.

"Well, I thought we could do it together," I said. "Maybe tomorrow after school?"

"Can't we do it today?" Olivia asked.

"I'm working on my science report with Katie," I explained, and Olivia pouted.

"Okay," she said, with a long, drawn-out sigh. "I guess I'll have to wait."

If Olivia was trying to make me feel guilty, it didn't work. There was no way I was going to back out on Katie.

So that afternoon I was happy when Katie got out at the bus stop with me. Eddie was home, and he had cookies and milk on the dining room table for us. (My mum is the healthy snack person in the house, but Eddie is happier with a cookie than a carrot.) I got out my laptop, so Katie and I could work on our reports.

"I was thinking about what you said on the bus this morning," Katie said. "About Ethan. I feel so bad for you!"

"Thanks," I said. "He was totally awful!"

"But then I was thinking about Jake," Katie said. "He's better now, but he used to be really bratty sometimes, remember? Like that one time we were baking and he had, like, this tantrum because he wanted a cupcake and they weren't ready yet?"

I shuddered, remembering. "I didn't know a kid could be so loud."

"We should probably ask Emma, but I'm thinking that maybe little kids get better when they get older," Katie said. "And besides, your dad is just dating her, right?"

"I guess, but he really seems to like Lynne," I confided. "You should have seen him running around, doing everything. 'I'll get that!' 'I'll do that!' Like he's totally in love with her."

"Or maybe he's just being extra polite," Katie suggested.

I sighed. "I hope so," I said. "If not, I'll just buy a pair of earplugs."

Then I switched on my computer. "So, we need to find pictures of the endocrine system, right?"

"No, I want to do a report on dinosaurs!" Katie said, using a little kid's voice.

I started to laugh. "No, Katie, today we need to do a report on the endocrine system," I said, using my best dad impression.

"No!" Katie yelled. "Dinosaurs! Dinosaurs! Dinosaurs!"

Eddie stepped into the dining room. "Wow, you girls are really excited about your homework, aren't you?" he asked, and Katie and I started cracking up.

Katie totally made me feel better about everything, just like she always does. Which is just one more reason why I will always, always, always be her friend.

CHAPTER 15

Losing My Patience

The next day I kept my promise to Olivia, and we stayed after school to decorate her locker. I brought all the supplies we needed, like scissors and double-stick tape for the wallpaper, and a special hook for the mirror that wouldn't ruin the wallpaper (like mine was).

There were still kids in the hallway, people who don't take the bus or people who stay for after-school activities, and a lot of them were curious about what we were doing.

"Okay, so first we need to take everything out," I said, which wasn't going to be easy because even after only a few days, Olivia's locker was a total mess. I started taking out crumpled-up papers, but Olivia just stood there with her back against the locker next to hers, watching people go by.

"Those girls look totally cool," she said, nodding to two girls who walked past.

"Oh, I guess," I said. "They're a grade above us. I don't really know them."

Then this girl Hanna from our grade walked up.

"Hi, Olivia," she said. "What are you doing?"

"Mia and I are totally redecorating my locker," she said. "We, like, designed it from scratch. It's going to be soooo cool."

I noticed that Olivia said "we," which was pretty annoying. It was also kind of annoying that she wasn't actually doing any work. So I dumped a bunch of rubbish in her arms.

"Here, throw this out," I said.

Olivia stuck her tongue out at me in a sort of funny way and went to throw out her rubbish. I piled her books and makeup boxes onto the floor and then got to work measuring and cutting the wallpaper. While I worked, Olivia just kept talking and talking.

"I mean, those BFC girls don't seem so bad," she was saying. "Maybe one day we could sit with them, you know?"

"Count me out," I told her. "I've been there before, and it didn't work out, remember?"

Olivia acted like she hadn't heard me, and she just kept talking about this cool outfit that Callie wore yesterday and wondering what Callie's closet looked like. Then she started talking about Emma's brothers.

"Matt Taylor is sooo cute," she said. "You guys must see him all the time when you make cupcakes, right?"

"Sometimes," I replied.

"And I heard Emma's oldest brother, Sam, is totally gorgeous," Olivia went on.

"Definitely," I agreed. I was too busy to feel chatty. Every time I tried to get Olivia to help, she found a way to get out of it. Like, when I asked her to put the double-sided tape on the back of the wallpaper, she kept saying, "Oh no, I can't get it to go on straight! You'd better do it, Mia. I'd ruin it."

Basically, I ended up doing the whole thing myself. When it was done, it looked pretty great. The light looked cool shining on the mirror, and the wallpaper was totally hot. Plus, I had found these strands of plastic jewels, and I strung them from the top shelf so that they dangled down. The whole effect was very cool.

"Mia, this is ah-may-zing!" Olivia cried when it was all done. She started snapping pictures with her phone. "My old friends are not going to believe this. Thank you sooooo much!"

So far, I had been shy about asking Olivia for the money for the locker stuff. But she seemed so happy that I figured this was a good time to bring it up.

"So, the forty-one dollars . . ." I said. "I kind of used my shoe savings to get your stuff, so if you could get it back to me soon . . . like tomorrow, maybe? It's actually forty-one dollars and thirty-six cents. But I don't care about the change."

"Oh, of course!" Olivia promised. "I'll bring it in tomorrow, I swear!"

But Olivia didn't. When I got off the bus and walked up to her, I said, "So, Olivia, did you remember the money?"

"Oh my gosh, Mia, I'm soooo sorry!" she said. "I totally woke up late this morning because my mum didn't wake me up, and I, like, rushed out. Tomorrow, I promise."

"Oh, okay," I said, trying to hide my disappointment. After all, she had an excuse.

Then when we were in registration, Olivia did that thing where she made me feel sorry for her. She turned to look at me with big, sad eyes.

"So, you know, Mia, I keep hearing you and

109

Emma and Alexis and Katie talk about that party," Olivia said.

"Yeah, well, we're baking a lot of cupcakes for it," I explained.

"Well . . . it's just . . ." She did that pouty lip thing again. "I haven't been to a single party since I moved out here. It's soooo depressing. I feel like such a loser, you know? So I was wondering if maybe you could ask Emma if I could come."

"Well, we're not really hanging out at the party," I said hesitantly. "We're sort of working."

"I know you guys don't want me in the business, so don't worry about that," Olivia said. "But I'll come and help and do whatever. Come on, we'll have fun."

"Well . . ." I wasn't sure how my friends were going to feel about this.

"Oh, please, Mia?" Olivia asked, making a supersad face, the kind Jake uses on us when he wants an extra cupcake. "I really need to make some new friends in this town."

"Okay, I'll ask," I promised, even though I regretted the words as soon as they came out of my mouth. But it wasn't a terrible idea, really. It could be like a test, to see if Olivia fit in, in a Cupcake situation.

So registration went like it always does, and I went to my locker to get my maths book, which I had forgotten to take out before. I turned the corner and saw Callie, Maggie and Bella gathered in front of Olivia's locker.

"You will not believe what I did yesterday!" Olivia said, opening the door.

I wasn't sure if I heard right. What "I" did? Olivia hadn't done a thing!

"Ooh, Olivia, this is fabulous!" Maggie squealed. "Look at that wallpaper!"

"I love the mirror," Callie added.

"Yes, and I even put in a light so I can do my makeup," Olivia bragged. She didn't even mention my name! Can you believe that?

"Olivia, you totally have to decorate my locker for me," Maggie said.

"Me too," Bella added.

"That would be fun," Olivia said. "I'll start coming up with some ideas."

How is she going to do that? I wondered. But I guess that's her problem!

Anyway, I had to go to my lesson, so I walked past Olivia's locker and waved.

"Hi, Olivia. Showing off your new locker?" I asked.

A guilty look crossed Olivia's face, and I knew she was wondering how much I had heard.

"Um, yeah," she said.

"See you later," I said, and walked away. I was starting to wish that I hadn't promised her I'd ask about Matt and Sam's party.

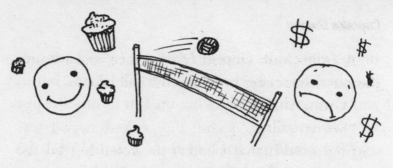

CHAPTER 16

From Good to Bad Again

That afternoon we went to Katie's house after school for a Cupcake meeting. Katie was kind of in a bad mood because Ms Chen had announced today that we were going to play volleyball for a few weeks.

Katie is a fast runner, but she's a terrible volleyball player. Whenever a ball comes to her and she hits it, it goes all over the place. For a while, she had a horrible time playing volleyball, but it's been a little better because Emma, Alexis and I are all in P. E. with her. So when we were playing, we made sure to run up and help her whenever the ball came her way.

Of course, we couldn't help her when she served the ball. I don't think she ever gets it over the net or on the right side. George Martinez (who I am sure likes her) teases her and calls her Silly Arms, but in a nice way, which cheers her up. But mostly she just hates volleyball.

"If I could go back in time, I would find the inventor of volleyball and convince him to keep his game to himself, so it wouldn't torture kids like me," Katie said as we were sitting around her kitchen table. She had her head in her hands and looked superbummed.

"I'm not sure if anyone actually invented volleyball," Alexis said thoughtfully. "I mean, it's basically just hitting a ball back and forth. I bet cavemen did that."

"With what? Rocks?" Emma asked. "I don't think cavemen had volleyballs."

"You know what I mean," Alexis protested.

"Don't worry, Katie. It's only for a few weeks," I assured her. "Plus, we're in your class now, so we can make it fun."

Katie sighed. "I will never use the words 'volleyball' and 'fun' in the same sentence."

Alexis brought us back to business, as usual. "So, we need to make up a schedule for the party on Saturday. We're baking on Friday night, right?"

"Right," Emma said. "Mum was wondering if

we could do it at one of your houses, because she needs to get our house ready for the party."

"We can probably do it here," Katie said.

"And what about the shopping?" Alexis asked.

"Mum and I are going to get everything tomorrow night," Emma replied. "We have to go shopping for the party, anyway. I'll bring it all with me on Friday."

Alexis gave us each a sheet of paper. "I printed out a copy of the final shopping list. I need everyone to check it and make sure we're not forgetting anything."

We all studied the list for a minute. Katie spoke up first.

"Looks good to me. But maybe we should put down that we specifically need creamy peanut butter. Chunky won't work so well."

Emma nodded and wrote on her list.

"I think it's fine," I added.

"All right," Alexis said. "So we bake, decorate and pack on Friday night. The party starts at three, so we should probably get to Emma's by one or two to set up."

"We should probably put on the chocolate basketballs on Saturday," I said. "They might get soggy if we stick them in the icing the night before."

"Okay, so then we'll get there at one thirty?" Alexis asked, looking at Emma.

"That's fine," Emma replied. "I'll double-check with my mum."

It looked like we had a plan, which meant our meeting was about to end, and I still had something to bring up. I was definitely nervous about it.

"So, I need to ask you guys something," I said. "I know we don't want Olivia in the business, and I get that. But she feels really left out, and she asked if she could help with the party. She doesn't want money or anything, she just wants to come and hang out. She's lonely."

Katie started chewing on her finger and didn't say anything. Emma looked at Alexis, and then Alexis spoke up.

"I don't know, Mia," she said. "I mean, does she really want to hang out with *us* or just you? She doesn't seem very interested in the rest of us."

"I know, you said that before," I said. "But maybe it's because she doesn't feel welcome because we have this club and she doesn't belong to it. Listen, I know she's not perfect, but she doesn't have anyone else at the school to hang with."

"Well, if she wants to help . . ." Emma said hesitantly. "I guess I could check with my brothers to make sure it's okay . . . since it's their party."

"Do we really have to?" Katie whined. "I mean, we sit with her every day at lunch. Isn't that good enough?"

Suddenly I felt a little angry and fed up.

"Why is hanging out with Olivia such a big deal for everybody?" I asked. I looked right at Katie. "It's, like, every time I want to make a new friend, you try to sabotage it. I'm not Callie, Katie. I'm not going to dump you."

Katie looked really stunned. Alexis and Emma exchanged a look, but didn't say anything.

"I'm going to text Eddie to pick me up," I said, and I walked outside. I didn't like feeling this way. Mostly, I felt confused. Why couldn't everybody just be friends? Why did it have to be so complicated?

It also bugged me that I was sticking my neck out for Olivia while I was kind of mad at her too. It definitely was not cool of her to tell people that she had decorated the locker herself. And she still owed me that forty-one dollars!

I texted Olivia that night.

Sorry 2b a pest, but I no how hard it is 2 remember things in the am. Can you bring in the money 2mrw?

117

She replied right away.

I.M. So Sorry. Keep forgetting! 2mrw for sur.

Tx! I typed.

I hoped she would remember this time. Because I really didn't like how things were going.

I was kind of mad at Olivia. I was kind of mad at Katie. Emma and Alexis were annoyed with *me*. Unless I could figure out how to work things out, I wasn't going to have any friends left in Maple Grove at all!

CHAPTER 17

Did She Really Do That?

I got another text that night, from Emma.

Matt & Sam say Olivia can come.

Tx! I typed back. She will be excited.

I thought about texting Olivia, but I figured I could just tell her in person at registration. I knew how happy she would be. So maybe things were working out after all. I mean, Emma could have lied and said her brothers didn't want Olivia to come. So maybe my Cupcake friends were finally coming around about Olivia. (Or Emma and Alexis were, at least.)

So the next morning I decided to face the day

with a positive attitude. I was worried that the bus ride with Katie would be awkward, and at first she was a little quiet, but luckily, the new season for this cooking competition show we both like had just started, so we talked about that for the whole ride. It was obvious we both wanted to put the argument we had the night before behind us.

Then when I got to registration, I talked to Olivia.

"So, you can help at the party on Saturday," I said. "Can you get to Emma's house by one thirty?"

"Ooh, Mia, thank you!" Olivia said, practically knocking over her desk to hug me. "Just text me her address, and I'll be there. Oh my gosh, I'm not sure what to wear. Can I come over to your house today to see if you have anything I can borrow?"

I mentally went through my schedule in my head. "Um, sure," I said. "Meet me by my bus, okay? We're just going to wear team shirts and jeans to go with the sports theme. But maybe we can think of some cool ways to accessorise."

Olivia nodded, but I could tell she wasn't really listening, and instead she was mentally going through my closet.

"Maybe I can borrow that cute skirt you have

with the ruffles," she said, mostly to herself. "I have a shirt that would go great with that."

I noticed Olivia didn't say anything about paying me back the money, and I felt weird asking her again. So I let it slide. If she brought it with her, I could always get it from her after school at my house.

In P. E. Ms Chen made me and George team captains. I made sure to pick Katie, Emma and Alexis for my team. George picked Olivia for his team before I had a chance. When Ms Chen wasn't watching, one of us Cupcakers switched places with Katie, so that she would never have to serve. I could tell that she was grateful, and it made me feel good.

When the game was over and we all walked to the locker room, Olivia walked up to me.

"Oh my gosh, now I know why George calls Katie Silly Arms," she said. "She looks totally ridiculous out there! I'm surprised she didn't whack you in the face."

I stopped walking. "Olivia, Katie's really sensitive about that. George can tease her because they've been friends for a long time."

Olivia shrugged. "I'm just saying. It's sooo obvious because she's such a klutz!"

We have lunch right after P. E. and I thought Olivia would spend the whole time talking about

Matt and Sam's party and what she was going to wear. But when I walked into the cafeteria, I was surprised to see Olivia sitting at the BFC table!

Maybe she's just talking to them about something, I thought. I bet she'll move over to our table in a minute.

But I unpacked my hummus and crackers and carrot sticks, and Katie unpacked her P-B-and-J, and then Emma and Alexis came to the table with trays of spaghetti and meatballs. Olivia stayed at the BFC table. I glanced over and saw that her lunch bag was open and she was eating sushi.

Alexis noticed too and raised an eyebrow.

"Well, that's interesting," she said. She looked at me. "Did she tell you she was changing tables?"

"No," I admitted. "But I guess she's free to sit wherever she wants, right? I mean, it's good that she has other friends, right?"

I believed what I said, but at the same time I was kind of hurt. I mean, I thought I was Olivia's best friend at the school. So why wouldn't she at least tell me she was sitting with the BFC? And was it permanent?

It's just lunch, I told myself. *No big deal.* And in a way, it was nice that she wasn't sitting with us. Katie was a lot more relaxed and Alexis wasn't rolling her eyes or shooting looks at Emma when she thought I couldn't see her.

After school, I waited outside the bus for Olivia, so we could go to my house like we planned. I waited until every single person got on the bus, but there was no sign of Olivia anywhere. Then when the bus driver said, "Time to go, Mia," I had no choice but to get on the bus.

Katie gave me a quizzical look.

"Olivia was supposed to take the bus with us," I explained. "But I don't see her."

"Maybe because she's with them," she said, pointing out the window, and I looked over her shoulder to see Olivia walking down the street with Callie, Maggie and Bella.

"Oh," was all I said, because I wasn't sure what to say. I felt even more hurt than I did at lunch.

Then I waited to hear what Katie would say, because she could have said something like, "Wow, she dumped you" or something like that. But Katie is too nice to say something like that. So she said, "Maybe she just forgot."

"Yeah," I said, thinking of the forty-one dollars. "She forgets a lot of things."

I was starting to think Olivia might not be a silver friend or even a bronze friend. And then I got even madder at her later, when I was doing my homework and Mum came home from a meeting in the city.

"Mia, you're not going to believe this," Mum said after she bent down to give me a kiss on the head. "I was walking past the Kara Karen store, and they're having a forty-percent off sale this weekend! I think you have enough to pay for your half now, don't you? I'll take you on Sunday."

I quickly did the math in my head. I definitely had enough . . . except for the fact that I had laid out that money for Olivia's locker.

"Well, kind of," I said. "I used part of my money to buy stuff when I redecorated Olivia's locker. She said she would pay me back, but she keeps forgetting."

Mum shook her head. "Mia, that's not right," she said. "It was very nice of you to help out your new friend, but she needs to pay you back."

"I asked her yesterday," I said.

"Then ask her again," Mum said firmly.

I cringed at the thought, but I knew Mum was right.

"You know, Mia, I have some concerns about Olivia," Mum said, sitting down next to me. "This business of forgetting to pay you back, when she knows how much you want those shoes. She doesn't seem as . . . well, as nice as your other friends."

For once, I didn't have the heart to defend Olivia. Mum was right.

"I know," I said. "It's just . . . She was new, and I didn't want her to feel weird or alone or anything."

"And that's one thing I love about you, Mia," Mum said. "You have such a good heart. Helping out Olivia was the right thing to do. But if she's not being a good friend to you, then you don't have to remain friends with her."

I thought about Olivia ditching me for the BFC today. "She might have already found some other friends, anyway," I told her.

I didn't know what felt worse – realising I might have lost a new friend or knowing that the Kara Karen shoes were in my grasp, but I couldn't get them. I decided to text Olivia again that night.

What happened after school?

Oh no! Totally spaced. Callie asked me to walk home with BFC, she replied.

I noticed that the word "sorry" was completely absent from her text.

125

So those shoes I want are on sale, I typed. Can u pls bring in the £ 2mrw?

K, Olivia texted back, and she didn't say anything else.

The next morning I just asked Olivia outright, "So, do you have the money?"

She immediately got defensive. "Come on, Mia, chill out! I've got a lot on my mind, you know? I'll bring it on Saturday."

"That would be good," I said. "Because I need the money on Sunday."

"Okay, okay," Olivia said, acting really dramatic about it. "It's not like I borrowed a million dollars or anything."

I couldn't wait for the day to be over, so I could go to Katie's and make cupcakes. But instead of going quietly, the day dragged on. And then P. E. was a nightmare.

We have, like, more than thirty kids in our P. E. class, and Ms Chen divides us into two groups to play volleyball at the two nets set up in the gym. Then she picks two people from each group to pick team members (four teams, two nets), so there's eight people on a team.

Anyway, on Friday I was in a group with all of my Cupcake Club friends, as well as Olivia and Maggie and Bella. Ms Chen picked Olivia and Wes Kinney to be captains.

Olivia got to pick first, and she picked me. Then she picked Maggie and Bella next, and then some boys. Emma and Alexis got picked for Wes's team. And then it came down to two people: Katie and Jacob Lobel, who's the shortest kid in our whole class.

It was Olivia's turn, and I was sure she was going to pick Katie. But instead she pointed to Jacob.

"I'll take Jacob," she said.

I couldn't believe it. Then Wes made it worse, because he groaned and said, "Oh, great, we're stuck with Katie!" On our team, Maggie and Bella started to crack up.

I was really angry this time.

"Why did you do that?" I asked, pulling Olivia aside. "Katie's our friend. You should have picked her!"

Olivia shrugged. "I'm the captain. I'm supposed to pick the best players. We want to win, don't we?"

It was another perfectly reasonable-sounding Olivia excuse. Except this time I wasn't buying it.

"Some things are more important than winning," I said, and then I walked away.

CHAPTER 18

The Real Olivia

I was so relieved when school was over on Friday and we all headed over to Katie's for some cupcake baking. Her mum ordered pizzas, we cranked up the oven and the music on my iPod, and then we got down to the business of cupcake baking.

The whole process was kind of complicated because both kinds of cupcakes were filled with different things. First, we baked seven dozen vanilla cupcakes. Even though the basketball and swim-team cupcakes were different, they both started with plain vanilla cupcakes. At first we were going to make six dozen, but we agreed it's always good to make a few extra. While they cooled, we ate our pizza and talked.

I didn't want things to be tense between me and Katie anymore, so I just jumped right in.

"So, that wasn't nice what Olivia did in P. E. today," I said.

Katie shrugged. "That's all right. I'm used to being picked last."

"Well, I thought it was wrong, and I told her so," I said, because I wanted Katie to know. She smiled.

"Thanks, Mia."

"Anyway, it didn't matter because we beat you guys, anyway," Alexis pointed out. "So maybe Olivia's team-picking strategies aren't so great."

"Yeah, you thrashed us," I admitted, because it was true.

"Do you think she'll still come to the party tomorrow?" Emma wondered.

"I don't know," I answered honestly. "I'll try texting her later. I know she's been hanging with the BFC, but she really wanted to come."

When we finished our pizza, it was time to fill the cupcakes. Katie and Emma made some instant vanilla pudding from a box to fill the swim-team cupcakes. Alexis and I got to work on filling three dozen of the cupcakes with jam. We used Katie's cupcake injector, which is kind of like the cupcake plunger she bought, but instead of removing the cake, you fill the injector with jelly or whatever, and then you stick it into the cupcake and squirt the jam right into the middle.

It's kind of messy, and pretty soon, Alexis and I were laughing and getting jam all over the place.

"Hey, you're supposed to fill cupcakes with it, not paint with it!" Katie teased.

"Oh yeah, well, let's see how well you guys do with the pudding," I teased back.

Katie held up the bowl to show me the vanilla pudding inside. "So far, no spills," she said.

Looking at the pudding gave me an idea. "Oh my gosh, we should totally dye the pudding blue!" I cried. "Then when you bite into it, the pudding will kind of look like water."

"Nice! Plus, it will be a real surprise," Emma agreed.

Katie picked up a tube of gel colouring. "Blue it is," she said, and she added some drops and stirred until the pudding was a perfect shade of swimming-pool blue.

After both kinds of cupcakes were filled, we put peanut-butter icing on the jam ones and piped blue icing on the pudding ones to look like waves.

"Those peanut-butter cupcakes will look even better with the basketballs," I said.

Alexis slapped her forehead. "Oh my gosh, the basketballs!" she said. "We still need to make them."

I looked up at the clock, and it was already eight. "We can do them in an hour, I promise."

Emma had picked up some plastic chocolate molds with small circles. We melted orange-coloured chocolate pieces in the microwave, poured them into the molds, and then put the molds in the freezer until the chocolate got firm. Then we popped them out and used a toothpick dipped in dark chocolate to draw dark lines on each piece to look like a basketball.

"We can only do one side at a time," I realised as we carefully placed the chocolate pieces on a cookie sheet. "Otherwise, the lines on the other half will get smooshed."

Katie yawned. "Maybe we should do the other sides tomorrow."

We all agreed. "Definitely," I said. "That way the lines can set overnight."

The next day, Mum drove me to Katie's, so I could help her pack up the car with all our cupcakes, plus the chocolate basketballs. When we got to the Taylors' house, Alexis was already there, and

131

Emma's mum and dad were running around, getting everything ready. As soon as Katie and I placed the cupcake carriers onto the kitchen table, Matt walked up and lifted the lid.

"Dibs on the first cupcake!" he said, reaching for one.

Emma slapped his hand. "Not yet, Matt. Wait until the party starts."

"But it's my birthday," Matt argued. "I get special tasting rights."

Then Sam came into the kitchen. He looks kind of like Matt, except taller, and he was wearing his swim-team T-shirt.

"Matt's right," Sam said. "Come on, birthday rights."

It's easy to argue with Matt, but Katie and I both have a little crush on Sam. We looked at each other, and then at Emma.

She sighed. "Okay. One each."

I handed Matt a P-B-and-J cupcake. "It's not really done yet. It's going to have a basketball on top."

Matt took a big bite. "Awesome! Jam explosion."

"I've got pudding in mine," Sam said. "I bet that was your idea, right, Katie? You're cupcake geniuses."

Katie turned bright red. "It was Mia's idea to make the pudding blue."

"All right, enough!" Emma yelled. "Out of the kitchen! We've got work to do."

We got busy finishing the chocolate basketballs, and we were almost finished when Mrs Taylor ran into the kitchen. A few strands of hair had come loose from her ponytail, and she looked frazzled.

"Girls, I'm setting out all the food on the dining room table, and it's getting pretty crowded," she said. "So maybe you could just put out one tray of each kind of cupcake to start and keep them filled during the party."

Alexis nodded. "No problem, Mrs Taylor. We've got it under control."

Emma's mum gave us a grateful smile and then raced out of the kitchen.

We had the cupcakes set up in about an hour, and then we pitched in and helped Emma's mum and dad set up the folding chairs in the back garden. It was a slightly chilly day, but still sunny and warm enough to be outside.

"So, it looks like Olivia's not coming after all," Alexis remarked as we positioned the chairs around a large table.

"I guess not," I said. "She never answered the text I sent last night."

Then a football came sailing out of the sky and knocked over one of the chairs. We looked up to see a small army of teenage boys walking up the Taylors' driveway and into the back garden.

"Yo! Where's the party?" one of them yelled.

"Quick! Let's retreat to the kitchen!" Emma suggested, and we followed her without question. Mrs Taylor whizzed by us.

"What was I thinking? Two parties at once?" she asked no one in particular.

Then we heard a knock on Emma's back door.

"Hello? Emma?"

It was Olivia! Emma went to answer the door, and Olivia walked in.

"Your dad said you girls were in here," she said. "I hope I'm not too late."

None of us said anything right away, because we were all sort of stunned by Olivia's outfit. We were all dressed in jeans and T-shirts or sporty shirts, to go with the sports team theme. But Olivia had completely ignored my advice and was dressed up like she was going to a dance or something. She had on a black bubble skirt with pink polka dots, a black top with lace down the front, tights and heels.

Then I noticed – they weren't just any heels. They were *my* heels! Olivia was wearing the Kara Karen shoes!

"The shoes!" I blurted out, pointing.

"Aren't they fabulous?" Olivia asked, lifting up a foot so we could all see.

"Yes, I know they're fabulous, because I'm the one who told you about them," I said. "When did you get them?"

"Well, my dad took me into the city last night, and wouldn't you believe it, they were on sale! I couldn't resist," Olivia said.

I didn't know whether to scream or cry. I was sure Olivia had used the forty-one dollars she owed me to get those shoes. Alexis must have noticed the look on my face, and she quickly handed Olivia a tray of P-B-and-J cupcakes.

"Olivia, since you're here to help, would you mind seeing if the cupcake tray in the dining room needs to be refilled?" she asked.

Olivia made a face and stepped back. "I don't want to get icing all over my new shirt!" she said. "You guys are better dressed for that than I am. Besides, these shoes are really hard to walk in. The toes are so pointy!"

It was all I could do to keep from screaming.

Katie took the tray from Alexis. "I'll do it. The dining room is full of boys. I bet they've emptied both trays by now."

"Boys?" Olivia asked. She walked (or wobbled, is more like it) over to the doorway and peeked inside the dining room. Then she turned around and took the plate from Katie.

"That's okay, I'll do it," she said. "I'll just be extra careful."

She put one hand on her hip and walked into the dining room. We headed in after her to watch the scene unfold. Olivia strolled right up to Matt and Sam. They were talking with their friends and didn't notice her. Olivia began to twirl her hair.

"I heard you boys needed some more cupcakes," she said.

"Oh my goodness!" Alexis cried, turning to us. "Do you know what we're seeing? The rise of Sydney the Second!"

Katie, Emma and I gasped. I couldn't believe I hadn't seen it before.

"Well, she's not *exactly* like Sydney," Katie said. "But they do have some things in common."

"They're both mean," Alexis said.

"And boy crazy," Emma added.

"And underhanded," I said, thinking of how

Olivia bought the shoes. "And self-absorbed."

It was like I was seeing Olivia clearly for the first time. Every time she tried to make me feel sorry for her, she was just manipulating me. Olivia wasn't a silver friend or even a bronze friend. She was a totally fake, plastic friend.

Olivia pranced over with an empty tray. "Emma, your brothers are so adorable! They need more cupcakes. Can you get me a plate so I can bring them some more?"

"You can get them yourself, Olivia," Emma said. "They're on the kitchen table."

Olivia rolled her eyes. "Well, I didn't know I'd be, like, a waiter!" she huffed, and marched into the kitchen.

"What does she thinking 'helping' means?" Alexis muttered.

Olivia stomped back out with an annoyed look on her face. She still had one hand on her hip and was holding the tray on the other hand. She started wandering around and she must have been looking for Sam, but I had seen him take his plate of food outside.

Then all of a sudden . . . *Blam!* Olivia lost her balance in the shoes and fell forward. Matt was nearby, and he sprinted forwards and grabbed her arm, stopping her from hitting the floor. But the cupcakes went flying everywhere, and a bunch of them hit Olivia. She had a blob of blue icing on her forehead, and her new shirt was streaked with peanut-butter frosting.

CHAPTER 19

The Cupcaketeers: Together Again

"Oh nooooo!" Olivia wailed.

There was a big commotion as the boys scraped cupcakes off their jeans and picked up the fallen cupcakes from the floor. Then Matt yelled out, "Hey, it's not a party until somebody smashes a cupcake!"

Everybody started laughing, and Olivia's face turned red. She spun around and pointed at Katie.

"Hey, Silly Arms, you really need to control yourself!" she yelled.

The room got quiet, and Katie turned pale. I quickly stepped in.

"Olivia, Katie wasn't anywhere near you," I said. "You tripped over your pointy shoes. And calling Katie names is not cool."

Olivia looked furious. She wiped icing off her

shirt. "I don't get this club, Mia. I mean, you're just waitresses. This is not cool. Or fun. I'd rather hang out at the mall with the BFCs."

"No one is stopping you," I said evenly, and Olivia started to storm out with her head held high.

"Say, Olivia, when you have a chance, I'd really like that money you owe me," I called after her.

Olivia stopped and then turned around.

"You know, for all the stuff I bought when I decorated your locker. So I could buy the shoes," I said, pointing to her feet. "Those shoes I showed you. I think it's so great that we both have the same taste in decorating and fashion, don't you?"

"Um, whatever, I'll bring it next week," she said, and then she marched out the back door.

We were all quiet for a minute.

"Something tells me I won't ever get that money back," I said. "But honestly? Those shoes don't seem so fabulous anymore."

Then we all started to giggle.

"I'm sorry, but that was kind of funny!" Emma said.

"She had icing from head to toe!" Alexis said, shaking her head.

"Thanks for sticking up for me," Katie added.

"That's what friends do," I told her. "Listen,

guys, I'm really sorry about everything. I was just trying to be nice."

Katie hugged me. "You don't have to try. You *are* nice!"

"All right, let's end this love fest," Alexis said. "We have some cupcakes to clean up."

"I'll do it," I offered. "It's kind of my fault that Olivia was here."

"No way," Emma said. "We're a club. We do things together."

It didn't take long to clean up the mess, and pretty soon we were able to enjoy the party. There were two giant hero sandwiches and potato salad to eat, but while our cupcakes looked gorgeous, we waited until the party was over to have one. Luckily, we always make extra cupcakes, just in case something happens . . . like if someone drops a bunch on the floor! There were six cupcakes left over, so we each took one and retreated to the kitchen.

Alexis held out her cupcake. "A toast! To another successful Cupcake Club project!" she said.

"Hear, hear!" we all cried, and then we clinked our cupcakes together.

"And," Alexis said with a mischievous look in her eyes, "to getting rid of Sydney the Second at our lunch table!"

"I'll second that!" I cried. "To the four best Cupcaketeers – and the four best friends – ever!"

We clinked cupcakes again, and then we each took a bite. Mine was delicious – but the sweetest thing of all was that everything was good with my friends again.